The Essence of His Soul

MYA KAY

#BLP

Copyright © 2023 by Mya Kay

All rights reserved.

No part of this book may be reproduced in any form or by any electronic or mechanical means, including information storage and retrieval systems, without written permission from the author, except for the use of brief quotations in a book review.

This is a work of fiction. Names, characters, places, and incidents are either products of the author's imagination or used fictitiously. Any similarity to actual events or locales or persons, living or dead, is entirely coincidental.

B. Love Publications
Heart Piercing Swoon Worthy Black Love Stories

Visit bit.ly/readBLP to join our mailing list for sneak peeks and release day links!

B. Love Publications - where Authors celebrate black men, black women, and black love.

To submit a manuscript for consideration, email your first three chapters to blovepublications@gmail.com with SUBMISSION as the subject.

The BLP Podcast – bit.ly/BLPUncovered

Let's connect on social media!
    Facebook - B. Love Publications
    Twitter - @blovepub
    Instagram - @blovepublications

Other Books by Mya Kay

<u>*Storms of Love*</u>
Battles of Love
In Loving Bliss
Fumbled Your Heart
Love to the B Power
Love to the Baby Power
<u>*A Star-Studded Love*</u>

Celebrity Reviews for Mya's Writing

"Mya paints a very vivid and real-life emotional picture with every sentence. Her writing fills me with joy, fear, anger, anticipation and a host of other emotions that keep me reading on and rooting for her characters." – **Terri J. Vaughn, Award-winning Actress from** *The Steve Harvey Show,* *All of Us,* *Soul Food,* **and** *Meet the Browns*

"My goal as I travel the country and perform as a comedian is at some point to become a person's favorite comedian. After reading Mya K. collection of short stories, I can honestly say I have a new favorite author. In one word, Mya is Awesome. I hope you enjoy her work as much as I did." – **Rodney Perry, Actor/Comedian, Co-host from BET's The Mo'Nique Show, Actor** *Madea's Big Happy Family,* *Coming 2 America*

Acknowledgments

To my Lord and Savior, Jesus Christ: I'm honored to serve through my pen. May You always get the glory and may more souls come to the Kingdom because of my work.

Mom: Thank you for always supporting my dreams, even when they cause both of us pain. If only people knew. Love you deep.

This one is for the women who work hard and are labeled strong but would love nothing more than to find a safe space for their independence to rest. It's okay to be strong and still want to be loved.

Introduction

Note to Readers:

I pray God has been touching the depths of your heart and soul with my writing. These stories are meant to help women and men heal from their past hurts and rediscover love God's way. If you're waiting for your Kingdom spouse, trust God's timing and His power.

One

ESSENCE

AS I WALKED into the upscale tea and coffee shop, I looked around in anticipation. Mocha Tea & Trends had only been open for six months and it was the new rave in Old City. I'd heard of how popular this place had become, and being able to find a comfortable seat near an outlet wasn't an option. The smell of roasted hazelnut and fresh doughnuts hit my nose as I searched for a seat. I had two contracts to look over and I still had to finalize this next album.

I had to admit, any place that was able to get a parking lot attached to their establishment in downtown Philadelphia was definitely worth patronizing. I breathed a sigh of relief as I hurried over to the cute, brown armchair with an open outlet. The line was pretty long, so I dashed over to snag the seat. Plugging my laptop in, I got settled, then smiled when I saw a barista. I waved her over.

"How are you?" I said, slightly out of breath. "How does this work?"

"First time here?"

I nodded. She handed me a menu.

"My name is Kayla. So, you can stand in line or you can have me take your order, but there's an automatic gratuity added. Twelve percent."

"Sounds good." I skimmed the menu quickly. "I'll have the chamomile tea with ginger and lemon, and a grilled cheese seafood sandwich. I've heard about them."

Kayla grinned. "They are everything. Literally our top seller."

"Thanks, Kayla. Here's my card," I said, handing my newest credit card over to her as she typed my order in.

She looked down, then looked back up. "Oh my gosh. You cut your hair."

I squinted, trying to place her face.

"Have we met?"

"Uh, no, but I go to Temple and I'm studying music. My professor talked about you a few weeks ago when he discussed women with big roles behind the scenes in music. I was really impressed and kind of stalked your social media."

She looked down nervously.

Laughing, I unbuttoned my coat and got more comfortable. "Well, Kayla, I don't know what your plans are, but don't give up. We need all the black women we can get in this business."

"Do you think I could email you sometime? You know, just to ask a few questions?"

I pulled out my phone and opened my electronic business card. "Do you have your phone?"

She dug into her apron and scanned the QR code on my phone. "My professor is not going to believe this," she squealed, walking away. "Thank you so much."

I smiled. Leaning back against the seat, I thought about how ambitious I was studying finance when I went to Temple. I had dreams of taking over corporate America, working in real estate and managing large portfolios for major commercial real estate companies. But God had other plans. After graduation, I spent two years in commercial real estate while working part-time for my parents' ministry.

My father, Bishop Devon Taylor, wanted his baby girl to take over the accounting and finance department at the church, while leading the young adult ministry as well. I landed an internship at Philadelphia International Music Group with the intentions of helping Milton, the

CEO, with his residential rental properties, only to find my love for music.

Some would say it was always there. I sang in the choir and I definitely could arrange a song, but I never wanted to be a singer, nor did I have a desire to work in music, but Milton heard me giving one of his engineers a few tips during my lunch break, and the rest is history. Six years later and I had my own record label and music management company, Taylor Made Music Group.

As I let my laptop get some more juice, I continued checking out the decor and the setup of the place. The area where they held their showcases and open mics looked like one of the studios in my building, which was refreshing. I was a firm believer that artists should always feel like they're stepping on the biggest stage in the world, no matter where they performed. I could turn a closet into a million-dollar studio with materials from Michael's.

Picking up my phone, I scrolled through my text messages until I landed on my business partner's thread. Trish Renee was a former Billboard-charting, Grammy award-winning artist who rose to fame in the early 2000s. While she had put down the mic and removed herself from in front of the scenes, she had picked up the knowledge and business acumen, and together, we managed four singers, two of which we had just signed. She owned 50 percent of the management company and 25 percent of the label. I couldn't have asked for a better partner.

I looked up just as Kayla was walking back over. She set my plate and tea down, then took a seat next to me.

"I'm actually getting off shortly. I know you're busy, but is there any advice you can give me?" Her smile faded. "I really feel lost."

I looked down at her trembling hand, then reached out and touched it. "Relax. Listen, you're studying music and I think that's great, but what's the overall goal? Are you studying music theory or music history? To be in this business, you don't need a degree. You need a strong business-mind, thick skin and faith. Study what you love. If music isn't it, you can still win in the business."

She nodded. "Right. You studied finance?"

"Yep. This wasn't even the plan, but I can honestly say that my years studying finance and working two years in commercial real estate prepared me to run my own business. God opened this door. I never thought I would be in music."

Her eyes grew wide. "Really? That's insane. I guess I have some praying to do. It's not too late to switch majors."

I held my hand up. "Now, I'm not saying that. I'm just saying don't put all your eggs in the music basket. Most of my colleagues that produced some of your favorite artists have degrees in everything but music. Just take your time and choose wisely. The industry isn't going anywhere."

She took a deep breath, then pointed to my sandwich. "I don't want your food to get cold. I appreciate you more than you know." She stood up. "I'll email you soon."

"Please do. Be safe."

She waved at me as she walked backward toward the door. I tried to warn her, but it was too late. She'd already bumped into the tall brother who was chatting away on his phone.

"Kayla, you okay?" he asked.

"Sorry, Mr. Bishop. I should've been paying attention."

Bishop? Is that who I think it is?

"Call me Shane. I told you that already," he said, handing her the scarf she dropped. "See you at the showcase Saturday night."

"Good luck on your game tomorrow night," she shouted as she exited.

Shane Bishop. It was him. I watched as he walked to the back, probably to a secluded, private area where he couldn't be disturbed, then turned my attention back to my meal. Picking up the sandwich, I sank my teeth into it and moaned. Literally. This was certainly heaven on a plate.

* * *

AN HOUR LATER, I was typing away on my laptop, working through my second quarter goals. It was already the second week of March and I felt behind. It was silly for me to think that way, but as a woman in music, I was always going to feel behind. One of my goals this year was to win the ASCAP Writer of the Year award. It was one of the biggest awards for songwriters and Kandi Burruss had been the first black woman to receive it.

I opened up another tab on my computer, then typed in Winter Daze website. I smiled as the soft tone of her syrupy voice filled my AirPods. She was my Neo-soul butterfly, and her new website was coming along beautifully. Trish and I signed her six months ago and her second single was just about ready to drop. As I turned down the music, I thought about how we'd been in the lab working hard. She was probably going to be our breakout artist of the year.

"I can't believe this. You really think I can find an artist of that caliber in two days?"

Me and a few of the other patrons looked up. The man who had been taking orders when I first walked in was now on the phone, going back and forth with someone.

"So, what does that mean? This is a celebrity establishment and you and I both know I won't be able to find a celebrity singer in two days. Everyone is booked, which is why we booked your artist."

I leaned up, zoning in on his conversation. *He needs an artist.* I looked back down at Winter's website and smiled. Closing my laptop and pushing it to the side, I grabbed my phone and stood up. Walking over to the counter, I stood, poised and ready as the gentleman wrapped up his call.

"This is crazy," he said. "Oh. I'm so sorry. Did you guys hear all of that?"

He looked around me at the other patrons. I turned and looked with him, watching everyone get back to whatever they were working on, with a few of the patrons snickering and shaking their heads. I turned back to him.

"Don't worry about it," I said. "Besides, I think I can help."

He raised an eyebrow. "Don't play with my emotions."

"Never."

"What do I have to do? And how much will it cost me?"

"My name is Essence Taylor," I said, reaching my hand out.

"Baylock Manson," he said, holding his hand up. "Don't ask. I'm the manager here."

I smirked. "I kind of figured that. I own Taylor Made Music Group, a label and management company for artists. My new artist, Winter Daze, is about to release her newest single and she just so happens to be available this Saturday night."

He shook his head. "Listen, Dear, we had Shailene booked for this Saturday. People are expecting a Grammy award-winning artist who has four hits on the radio right now, not some local has been."

I bit my bottom lip to keep from saying something smart.

"First, Winter's last single went viral on TikTok, and so do all her covers, including the one of Shailene's single, *Better Times*."

I pulled up my TikTok and went to Winter's page. I found the video of her singing Shailene's top hit of last year. I disconnected my AirPods, hit play and handed Baylock the phone. I could tell by his open mouth he hadn't been expecting that. As he continued staring at the phone, I already had Winter's outfit planned in my mind. He would say yes. He had no other choice.

"She's flawless," he whispered. "Oh, Sweets. Do you forgive me? Why isn't she bigger?"

I grabbed the phone back. "We're working on it, and is this how you treat people who you need a favor from?"

He chuckled, then grabbed my hand. "I'll do anything."

I raised an eyebrow. "Anything?"

"Oh, Lord. Listen, the owner is the one with all the money. I'm on salary."

"Honestly, just promise me the house will be full and pay my artist what you were going to pay Shailene."

"Okay, now hold up. She's good, but she isn't that good."

If he thought I was going to let Winter perform for free, he had another thing coming. However, I realized Shailene charged $50,000 per performance, so I knew I couldn't ask for that much.

"Twenty thousand. Paid upfront, due to the last-minute request."

He crossed his arms. "How many songs?"

"An hour's worth. Two exclusives."

"Ninety-minutes and we have a deal."

Sighing, I stuck out my hand. "Deal."

I texted Trish and Winter in our group chat. I would have to draw up a contract and have Winter sign it electronically, but this was a good look. I'd heard about the once a month celebrity performances they held here, charging folks $300 just to enjoy the show. This place was exclusive to an elite group of celebrities during that weekend, and most people who came looked at $300 like it was toilet paper money.

"So—"

"Is my manager giving you a hard time?"

I looked up from my phone to see who had cut me off. It was a different voice, and when I saw who it belonged to, I was speechless. It was Shane Bishop.

"Your manager?" I asked.

Baylock leaned on the counter. "I told you it was the owner that has all the money, Honey."

"Wait, *you* own Mocha Tea & Trends?"

He laughed. "Why is that a shock?"

"Maybe it's because you're an NBA player for one of the hottest teams in the league, three-time MVP and an All-Star four times. That doesn't really line up with being a tea and coffee shop owner."

"Well, coffee is where the money is. So, here I am," he said. He looked at me. "Your hair is pretty."

Baylock snapped his fingers. "I meant to say that, but we were planning. Shane, she just saved us."

As Baylock filled Shane in, I looked at the cross tattoo on his neck. While I was around stars all the time, Shane's presence was definitely strong. As he talked, I watched his lips move. He seemed to lick them after every few words. When he turned his attention back to me, I couldn't help but notice how straight and white his teeth were. His goatee was neatly trimmed, and his eyes were the nicest deep brown I'd ever seen.

"Uh, earth to Essence," Baylock said, snapping his fingers in front of my face. "Girl, you good? You checked out on us for a minute."

I shook my head. "Sorry about that. Uh, thank you for the compliment. I actually just cut and colored it, so it's nice to know it's being noticed."

Shane winked at me. "I doubt you have a hard time getting noticed. You're gorgeous."

Baylock looked at me, then at Shane. "I think I need to go restock and check on the customers. Essence, let's talk tomorrow to discuss particulars."

"Of course. I'll have the contract done by then. Three o'clock work?"

"Perfect," he said, air kissing my cheeks. "Oh, and Honey, those jeans are screaming wonders on you. I love me a thick chick."

He disappeared into the back. Shane and I looked at each other and burst out laughing.

"Sorry about that. Baylock can be a lot."

I flagged him off. "Please. He's great. I'm just glad I could help."

"You have to let me repay you," he said, licking his lips again. "I have a game tomorrow, but I'll be here Saturday. I'd love to take you out for brunch before the show."

I opened my mouth to reply, then closed it. I'd done this before, except it was a baseball player. It lasted all of three weeks. As much as I prayed for a husband, I wasn't desperate, and I didn't do drama.

"Listen, I'm doing this for my artist. This is a good look for us, so no need to repay. I'm glad you host opportunities like this, but you should open it up to newer artists."

"I usually let Baylock and our events manager handle all of that."

I shrugged. "Makes sense." I looked over toward my laptop. "Well, look, it was nice meeting you. I have to get back to work, especially since I have forty-eight hours to get my client ready."

I turned and walked away before he could speak. If I was being honest, I had to get away from him before I broke my vow to God. I hadn't had sex in two years, and I planned on keeping it that way until I was married, but Shane definitely had a magnetic energy about him that felt peaceful. I also noticed he wasn't as cocky as I thought he'd be.

Nonetheless, I had enough men sliding in my DMs and hitting on me at Hollywood parties and music events and I didn't need any distractions. It wasn't always easy waiting on God, but I'd been through too much with my ex, Dixon, and reputation was everything in this industry. I had enough rumors to dodge just being the daughter of Bishop Taylor and being a music mogul who didn't take no stuff. I refused to lose focus.

Two

SHANE

I SHOT the ball a few more times, making sure my jump shot was tight for tonight's game. It was only five in the morning and I had to be at practice at noon, but this season had been rough, and I knew my team was depending on me. Here it was, March, and we only had eight games left for the regular season. We'd have to win all of them in order to make the playoffs, but our center and other guard were out for major injuries, leaving me, the point guard, and our power forward, carrying the weight of the team on our shoulders.

As I shot the ball again, I couldn't help but think about Essence. When she walked away from the counter yesterday, I wanted to call out to her, but I stopped myself. After what I'd gone through a year ago with my ex, Rayna, I wasn't pressed over any woman. What was meant to be, would be. I could admit there was something about Essence that made me want to get to know her more. I asked Baylock about her, but all he could offer was stuff I could find on my own via Google.

I was impressed with her business credentials and thought it was interesting that she, too, was a PK. Yes, I was a preacher's kid. My parents, Pastor Lawrence Bishop and my mother, Shandra Bishop, were pastors at Lightway Missionary Baptist Church in Camden, New Jersey. They weren't the lead pastors, but they were a huge part of the pastoral team and were on salary at the church. Essence's parents, on the other hand, were what many would call Mega Pastors. Everybody knew Bishop Devon Taylor and First Lady Melissa Taylor.

Once I finished stalking her social media and her company website, it clicked how we had met. Before my mother was ordained a few years ago, she had a speaking engagement at a family conference in Miami. My father couldn't go, so I accompanied my mother. Since it was the off season, it worked out perfectly. I remember my mother talking to Essence's mother, who was actually the keynote speaker, and that was when we were introduced. It was crazy how I forgot about that moment.

Sure, I met a lot of women and, to be honest, I was bad with names, but to Baylock's point yesterday, Essence had a face and body nobody could forget. I was sure she could stand out in any crowd. What I loved about her visually, was that she wasn't your typical size-two model chick. She was thick and curvy, kind of like Chrissy, Jim Jones's girlfriend. Reading that her mother is half-Cuban explained her exotic features and that beautiful head of hair.

"Chill out, man," I said to myself. "You sound like a model scout."

Chuckling, I shot one last shot, then grabbed the bouncing ball to head inside. I needed to ground myself before I started my day. While I couldn't even remember the last Sunday I'd been to church because of my schedule, I never let a day go by without reading my Bible and I prayed. A lot. Prayer was the only other thing keeping me sane during the season. I was grateful to have a few teammates who also understood the power of prayer. Sometimes, we'd have Bible studies with the team chaplain while traveling.

I walked back inside my home, the lights coming on as soon as I entered. I grabbed a water from the fridge, then picked up my phone. I had time to listen to an audiobook, catch up on some sleep and eat a good, hearty meal before heading to practice. Just when I was about to turn the audiobook I'd been listening to on, my phone lit up. I smiled.

"What do you want? And why are you up so early?" I teased as soon as I answered.

"Well, hello to you, too, big brother. I miss you, too."

I shook my head. "Hey, love. What's going on with you?"

I sat down at my kitchen counter.

"Nothing much. Just called to see how you feelin' about tonight's game. This is a big one."

"Of course it is, Sahana. We need to win this game and every one we have left in order to make the playoffs. I can't believe Kid is out."

"Kid's always been the careful player. This injury is crazy."

I smirked. My sister's knowledge of basketball was ridiculous. I was surprised she never played with the way she knew the game.

"Yeah, well, to answer your question, I feel nervous. Excited. Concerned. This is a big game."

"At least you guys are playing Milwaukee."

"They've gotten better. Don't sleep on them."

I knew she was just being encouraging, but my first year in the league, I'd made the mistake of thinking Milwaukee wasn't that strong of a team. They beat us twice that season and I wasn't talking about by two points. I learned quickly to respect the game and the players, even if you didn't think their team was that dope.

"Enough about me, though. How's everything with you?" I asked, changing the subject.

My sister filled me in on how things were going for her as a trademark attorney. She was enjoying it and I was mad proud. She passed the bar her first time, which wasn't easy, and she found a job working with a strong trademark firm right here in Philly. Most people had to move to New York or somewhere else to get a good job their first year after taking the bar, but my sis snagged a great job.

"I'm proud of you, Sis. You really worked hard to get where you are."

"Thanks, Bro, but you're the superstar."

I took a deep breath. I hated when she did this. She had no idea how I wished there was more to me than just being a basketball player. I took this route because I was a natural at it. I just wasn't so sure it was fulfilling me the way I thought it would.

"The real superstar is the person who pursued what was in their heart and is walking in purpose," I said, then quickly added, "Have you talked to the 'rents?"

"You know we have to check in or they will."

I shook my head, but smiled. It could be annoying, but their love outweighed their sometimes overbearing ways.

"Listen, are you coming to the game tonight? I can leave your box tickets at will call."

"You know what, that's a great idea. I was going to keep working on some things for a client, but I need a break."

I stood up and started heading upstairs. I felt my basketball workout mellowing me out. It was nap time indeed. I could listen to the audiobook as I fell asleep.

"Sounds good. I'll leave two so you can bring a friend, but not a man."

She laughed. "Just for that, I'm going to call up this guy I'm seeing and see if he's free tonight."

I froze in place, my hand resting on my bedroom doorknob. "Sahana—"

"I'm grown. Get over it. See you tonight," she said, rushing me off the phone. "And maybe if you started dating again, you wouldn't be such a grump."

Click. She hung up. I chuckled, then put my phone on the charger.

My sister and I had one thing in common—we never seemed to choose the right partner. It was crazy because I was considered the "good guy" when it came to basketball players. By good guy, I mean I wasn't the type to lie down with just anybody and I was a one-woman man. Most of my teammates bragged about the many women they laid down with in a week or how they had a girl in every city. Now, I wasn't tooting my own horn. My teammates actually teased me for being a "goodie two shoes". I was no angel, but I'd be lying if I said I didn't think I'd be married by now.

And I almost was. When Rayna and I first met, I thought I finally knew what my father was saying when he would tell me how he fell in love with my mother. I proposed after eight months and we had even started pre-marital counseling. Things were going well, even with my busy schedule and her work as a model and actress. We fought for our relationship, making time for each other where most would just make excuses. We picked a date for our wedding, which was scheduled for six months after I proposed. I was okay with that.

Then, Rayna started acting weird as we got closer to the date. She pushed it back once, to two months later than the original date. I was okay with that. No pressure. But she grew more distant, started pushing me away and acting like I was some clingy dude who was sweating her. That was when the truth came out. I remember the conversation like it was yesterday.

"Rayna, what's going on? I can feel something is off," I said. "You've been acting weird for months now."

"Shane, everything is fine. Just because things aren't going the way you want doesn't mean something has to be wrong. Relax."

My jaw clenched when she said that. By then, I was sick of her playing me like I was some chump.

"Watch how you talk to me," I said. "I'm getting tired of you coming at me like I'm some boy with a teenage crush."

I could tell by the way she looked at me that my tone had caught her attention. I wasn't playing.

"Listen, baby, all I'm saying is I'm okay. Marriage is a big deal. I just want to make sure I'm really ready."

"Then why have you been canceling our counseling sessions? We've rescheduled the last four and you don't seem too excited to make the one we have scheduled now."

She paced the floor. By this point, she couldn't even look at me. I saw how nervous she was. She walked over to the bay window in her apartment and stared out into the city streets. When she turned back around, I knew. I knew the suspicion I'd been feeling for the last several months was true. I saw it in her eyes. She had someone else and it was written all over her face. She touched her belly, pressing my long, white button up against her stomach. I squinted, trying to make sense of it. Then, she dropped the bomb.

"It's not yours," she whispered.

I threw the lamp against the wall of her bedroom and walked out before I did anything else. There had been rumors flying around, but I ignored them because she gave me the same courtesy. I knew it wasn't easy dating a basketball player, so when girls slid in her DMs with the lies and the photoshopped pictures and she dismissed it because she trusted me, I felt I owed her the same respect. But I guess I should've considered the evidence.

It had been staring me in my face the whole time—ending our calls quickly, taking late-night phone calls and leaving the room, saying she was with her model friends only to change the story up and say they canceled at the last minute but she had hung out alone. All the signs were there.

Now, here I was, a year later and I felt I had just fully bounced back in the last few months. I kept asking myself how I missed it. Some men say they can feel the difference when their woman has been with someone else, but I guess I was naïve.

She banked on me being too busy to really check up. When we broke up, she was only six weeks pregnant, so there was no way I could've known on sight. She'd been ducking me so much that any morning sickness or other signs she'd been able to hide. I closed my eyes, trying to shake the bad memories away, but I knew that would always be a part of my story, no matter how much I wanted to forget it. I hadn't really dated seriously since. In fact, I just started dating again last month. If it wasn't for my dad and my therapist, I wasn't sure how I would've made it through that breakup.

Lying down on my bed, I let out a deep breath, then said a prayer before trying to get some rest.

"God, I know I should've waited on You when it came to love. I know You have someone for me and I'm willing to wait and see who it is. I know the guys tease me sometimes for being so serious with relationships, but I've seen what a healthy marriage looks like. My parents have thirty-five years in and I want that. Help me make better decisions with my love life, even if that means not dating at all until You say, 'that's her'. Help me wait on You. In Jesus's name, Amen."

Smiling, I turned over on my side and closed my eyes. When I saw her, I almost opened my eyes to fight the vision, but the peace I felt when her face popped into my head made me stay there. I didn't know if it was me or God trying to tell me something, but I had no problems visualizing Essence Taylor.

* * *

"WHOOOOOOOOO!" I screamed, jumping on another teammate as we filtered into the locker room. "Yeah, baby. We did it."

I couldn't believe we had won. By halftime, we were down eight points and I was nervous. I had a feeling we could come back strong, but Milwaukee wasn't playing tonight. I was no longer worried about the playoffs as much as I was before, I just wanted the NBA to know we weren't to be played with. We couldn't lose this game. And we didn't.

"You came in the clutch with those last three three pointers, Bro," my teammate, Reggie, said to me. "Killed it."

We did our special handshake and hugged. "Thanks, bro. Couldn't have done it without you."

I felt the celebration in the air as a few teammates popped open a couple of bottles of champagne. We were acting like it was the championship.

"Great job, team. What a way to come back after that first half," Coach Mills said. "I'm proud of you guys. We have to keep that up if we want to make it to the playoffs."

We all agreed in unison, then continued celebrating.

"Chima's is calling my name," Reggie yelled out. "Who's down?"

A bunch of roars filled the room.

Chima's was one of the best steakhouses in Philly and, of course, one of the best restaurants, period. It was the perfect place to celebrate.

"I'll call ahead and get you guys set up," Coach Mills said.

I watched as my guys continued to celebrate, but I thought about Essence again. I not only had a vision of her before I fell asleep, but I actually had a full-on dream. We were at a red-carpet event and she was alone on the carpet, taking pictures at the step and repeat. Then she looked back toward me and waved me over with her finger. I felt like I was floating on air as I made my way over to her. I took her hand in mine and we posed for pictures, then she turned to me and said, 'I love you'. I woke up in a sweat, wondering what the heck all of this meant.

"Yo, bro, you cool?" Kevell, another teammate, asked. "You seemed zoned out."

I laughed nervously. "Naw, I'm cool. Just happy we won. Processing."

He slapped my back, then headed to the showers. I leaned my head back against my locker and took a few deep breaths to calm my heart rate down. It was definitely still pumping.

"Bro, you did it," I heard a voice say.

I jumped up and grabbed Sahana in a big hug. "Thanks for coming, Big Head."

"Oh my gosh, you stink! And you're sweaty."

I looked over at the security officer, who had let her in. "Thanks for looking out."

He nodded.

"Listen, we're headed to Chima's to celebrate. You wanna come?"

"I have a coworker waiting for me. Let me see what she wants to do. I don't want to be around a bunch of testosterone alone."

"Agreed. Maybe you should call a few friends to even things out."

She grinned, then kissed my cheek. "Mom and Dad watched the whole thing. They are so proud of you."

I felt myself blushing. My parents came to a lot of the games, but of course, they couldn't make them all. It just felt good to know I made them just as proud as an athlete as they would've been if I'd become a doctor like they wanted.

"All right, bro. We'll meet you guys there," she said, breaking me out of my thoughts. "Love you."

"Love you more."

"Love you too, boo," I heard a voice say behind me.

I turned around and popped Reggie with my towel. "Don't play with me. You know Sahana is off limits."

"I know, I know. Just joking, bro."

I shook my head, laughing as I headed to the showers. I hadn't looked at my phone yet, but I was betting I had a bunch of notifications, DMs and missed phone calls. No matter what, there were certain people who still called to congratulate me on a win, even though they knew I wouldn't answer. It was virtually impossible to talk to anyone outside of the press after a game. I knew one thing. If I had gotten a certain somebody's phone number before she left the coffee shop, that would've been one call I would be anxious to take.

* * *

"YEAH, well, superman here decided he wanted to go on record for the most back-to-back three pointers in a game. Showoff," Kevell said.

Everyone shared a laugh at my expense, but I was cool with it. Three pointers weren't my strong suit, but I took every shot tonight. I looked back down at my phone, scrolling the page I was on and smiling at the same time.

"What the heck are you looking at? You've been staring at that phone since we sat down."

Toussaint, our center, leaned over and looked at my phone. I tried to cover it up, but it was too late.

"Shoot, I would be distracted by that, too. Who is she?"

I flinched at him calling her 'that', like she was an object, but I was busted, so I had to come up with something.

"Just another PK I ran into the other day."

"Let me see," Kevelle said.

I hesitated, then slowly handed him my phone. Our other teammates were at the other end of the table, laughing and howling over something else. I was glad only Toussaint, Kevelle and Reggie were nearby.

"Wow. Wow. And wow again. Is this you?" Kevelle asked.

I grabbed my phone back. "No. She came into Mocha Tea & Trends the other day and we talked. I remembered meeting her before after she left, so I looked her up."

"Did you get the number?" Reggie asked.

I shook my head.

"Wait. You let somebody that looks like that, leave your shop without getting their number? So, that means I can holla, right?"

For some reason, I was getting uncomfortable. I didn't really know Essence that well, but I felt my protective nature getting ready to take over.

"No. You can't."

I guess the tone in my voice told them how serious I was, because Kevelle quickly changed the subject.

"Yo, remember those baddies we hung with last weekend, in St. Louis? They want to meet us next week when we play in Missouri again."

As the fellas continued their conversation, I looked back down at Essence's profile page. I contemplated sending her a DM, but I didn't want to come off like a creep. I could just say something like: *It was nice meeting you and your next latte is on me*, but I didn't want to come off cheesy either. I thought about it for a few more minutes, then had an idea. She would appreciate this. I opened my DM, then sent the message, praying to God the whole time I typed.

Three

ESSENCE

I LAUGHED. Hard. If I didn't know any better, I would even say I was blushing. Of all the DMs I'd ever gotten with someone trying to holla, this one was it. He wasn't trying too hard and he wasn't coming off corny, he was just being him, I guess. I re-read it out loud as I waited in the car in front of my parents' home. I was spending the day with my mother and I needed to prepare myself mentally before I went in.

"Hey, beautiful. What do you get when you combine two PKs who work in different industries in entertainment, but stand on their faith no matter what? Four overbearing parents who wanted us to choose different careers, a bunch of clout chasers in our DMs and a lot of fake prayers from people who want to see us fail. Listen, I've been wanting to hit you up, but I wanted to make sure it would be worth your time. There's no point in beating around the bush, I'm captivated by you and I would do anything to hang with you for a day. Say yes and I'll make it worth your while. I need another PK to take this journey with me."

When I left Mocha Tea & Trends that day, I quickly recalled that we had met before. I literally almost forgot he was a PK until the memory popped into my head. His mother was such a sweetheart and I remember him being so protective of her. It was kind of cute seeing how he stepped into his father's shoes when he wasn't around. I would be lying if I said he didn't catch my attention then, but I was so focused, I brushed it off. There was one memory from the conference I'd never forget, though.

It was when my mother was preaching. I remember looking over at him. We were in the VIP section, of course, because we were the family members of the speakers. He hung onto my mother's every word, barely paying any attention to the women who were whispering around him. I saw him taking notes in a journal, not his phone, which definitely caught my attention. He was following along in a way that told me he was serious about his walk. When I turned my attention back to my mother, I remember how that image of him wouldn't leave my mind.

Now, here we were, a few years later and I still remembered that moment. I looked down at my buzzing phone. It was Trish. Tonight was the big night for Winter and everything was good to go. I was spending the morning with my mother, then for the rest of the day, it was about tonight's showcase at Mocha Tea & Trends.

"Hey, girl. What's going on?"

"I just wanted you to know that this new publicist for Winter is working wonders. She was able to get Action News and CBS 3 to come cover the showcase. This is major. And, I know you'll be with your mom and won't be taking calls, so I guess I should tell you now that we have to find a new outfit. I can't reach the stylist."

I shook my head. "Let's pull something she already has. I know that seems old, but she has quite a few outfits from previous red-carpet events she only wore one time. This is about exposure."

"That's what I suggested. I knew you would agree. I found someone last minute to help style her with something she already has, the makeup artist and hairstylist are good to go, and she'll be at the venue for sound check at four p.m. I know they're closing at two to prepare, which is perfect."

"I'm excited. I can't wait. I should get to you all by two. Love you, sis."

"Love you. See you soon."

I hung up the call just as my mother opened the door. I rolled down the window.

"Coming, Mama. Had a business call."

Rolling the window back up, I closed my eyes and whispered a prayer, then opened the door. To be fair, my mother, I could handle. It was Bishop Taylor who was an issue.

"Baby Girl," she said, as I stepped into the foyer. "Your hair looks beautiful."

We hugged. I held her close, appreciating the normalcy.

"Thanks, Mama. What did the doctor say about those headaches?"

She sucked her teeth. "You're just like your father. Business first."

"Always, but this is health business. It's important."

She flagged me off, then led me into the living room. "I'm fine. All the scans and MRIs came back fine. He said to take it easy and to try to lay off the coffee."

I looked down at the coffee table, which had coffee and danishes. She laughed.

"I mean, I haven't had any all week. Ask your father."

I smiled. My mother's sense of humor was something I could always count on.

"Ask me what?"

My father's deep baritone voice drifted into the room before he did.

"I was updating our daughter on my health."

He walked over to me and I stood up. "I told your mother not to do coffee today, but you know how she is." He grabbed my hand. "Hey, sweet pea. How are you?"

He wrapped me in a hug, then kissed my forehead. "I'm actually headed to a church meeting now. I'm glad you're here because she would want to go, and she doesn't need to be there."

"I agree," I said. "I'm good, Daddy. How are you?"

"Health wise, I'm great."

My mother stuck her tongue out at him.

"Ministry, business, everything is well. How's the business?"

I waited before responding. This was where we always butted heads. He never asked out of genuine concern. He was waiting for the day I brought home a bad report so he could say, "I told you so".

"Well, it's going good. We have a showcase tonight at Mocha Tea & Trends. My artist is actually getting paid pretty nice for this, so I'm excited."

"I've been meaning to get down there. I heard the seafood grilled cheese sandwiches are heavenly."

He walked toward the vestibule to grab his jacket from the closet. I swallowed, trying not to cry because he acknowledged everything but my accomplishment. He was more excited about a grilled cheese sandwich that my mother could probably make for him in her sleep.

"Have fun, my ladies. Love you both."

He walked over and kissed my mother, squeezed my shoulder, then left. My mother grabbed a cup and poured herself some coffee. I knew she was nervous because the coffeepot was shaking as she poured.

"I'll have tea, Mama."

I grabbed some lavender tea leaves and the hot water to make my tea. The silence in the room was thick.

"We saw Clayton the other day," my mother said.

I stopped pouring the water. "And?"

I made sure to keep my tone respectful, but I wanted no parts of this conversation.

"I'm just telling you we saw him. He asked about you," she said, without looking at me. "He really wants another chance to take you out."

"I'm good. I hope you didn't give him my number."

"I didn't."

I looked at her. "Daddy..."

She nodded. "I actually was on your side, although I like Clayton. I told him not to disrespect your privacy like that."

I was seething. My parents had been trying to hook me up with Clayton McCoy for the last four years. He was the son of Bishop Clayton, Sr. and First Lady Sandra McCoy. While he had a lot of great qualities, his desire to ask his parents 'how high' when they told him to jump and his traditional mindset of how a woman should operate were huge turnoffs. We went on one date four years ago and I vowed to never see him again. We never even finished the date. We made it through appetizers when he stated, "I'm looking for a woman that understands what it means to be on the arm of a man of God and whose willing to manage our household and ministry while I build the legacy and family name."

I laughed so hard, he actually got offended. I mean, did they even make women like that anymore? I'm not saying it's wrong, but most women I knew were business owners, or they led ministries with their husbands. That mentality was why my mother agreed with most of the decisions my father made and I refused to do that for any man. I needed someone who would respect that I have just as much purpose as he does.

"So, what's for brunch?" I asked, changing the subject.

I wasn't worried about Clayton. If he called, I had no problem putting him in his place.

* * *

WINTER HAD ALREADY KILLED her first three songs and the crowd was going crazy. I had to admit, Baylock knew how to throw an event. Not only was the décor and the ambiance lit, but the host, KB, knew how to get the crowd hype. The way she introduced Winter was fire. I couldn't wait to connect with her after and see if she would be available for any of Winter's smaller shows that we did in the city. Trish and I were sitting right in the front, singing along with Winter and making sure she knew that if nobody else was going to root for her, we were.

People said Philly fans were hard on the artists, athletes and anyone who was a public figure. I had to agree, but there were times they definitely surprised me. While this was an exclusive event for celebrities to have a fun night of entertainment without the distraction of fans, I asked Baylock to open up at least twenty-five tickets for anyone who wanted to come at a discounted price of $175. It was great to have celebrities watching you perform, but the truth was, it was the local bloggers and local people who created the buzz.

I knew most people wouldn't want to pay that much for one artist, especially someone who was still considered new, but they got the same deal—a full meal, two drinks, and entertainment. Winter's street team had also created some dope goodie bags everyone got for free. This was what it meant to invest in an artist before you would see returns. It was part of the game. By now, Trish and I were standing up, dancing, and most of the crowd was grooving right along with us. I was in a zone.

It wasn't until I looked toward the counter and saw him staring at me that I stopped moving. How long had he been watching? I looked away, then continued dancing. When we first arrived, I admit I looked around for him, but when I didn't see him, I figured he was getting rest for tomorrow night's game. He said he would be here, but I wouldn't have blamed him if he didn't come. He played his behind off Thursday night. He deserved a break.

"Okay, okay. Isn't our girl Winter Daze killing it?" KB said, walking out as Winter walked off the stage, blowing kisses at everyone. "I was adding these songs to my playlist as she was singing, but uh, excuse me, Ms. Manager, right there..."

She pointed at me. I laughed.

"We need y'all to stop playing with our emotions and get those other songs recorded. I couldn't find them on Spotify, and Honey, I ain't switching to iTunes if that's where they at."

The crowd roared.

"We got you," I said loudly. "Promise."

She pointed at me. "All right, y'all. You heard her. Imma give you two weeks. I should be done with my boyfriend by then and Imma need those last two songs for sure."

More laughter filled the room. I was having a ball. KB continued sharing a few jokes, then she let everyone know it was intermission time. We had a twenty-minute break, then Winter would close out with the exclusive tracks nobody had heard yet. I headed to the green room to talk to her. I knew she was nervous. We had written these songs a few months ago and it had taken her some time to become comfortable singing them. She had never sung these types of songs before. Today, would be the first time she was trying something new and we had some push back when Trish and I first approached her with it.

"You in a rush to get somewhere?" I heard a voice behind me say.

Without even turning around, I knew who it was. Smiling, I turned to face him. My words got caught in my throat. I had a smart response, of course, but I hadn't expected him to look this good. The way his eyes looked under the lights where we stood were more mesmerizing than the first time we had met here. I saw his muscular frame under his long-sleeve Eddie Bauer shirt. Even the way his jeans laid was nice. He wasn't too flashy, but he definitely stood out.

"Hey, Shane," a woman said, walking past us to head to the bathroom.

"Hi," he said, sheepishly, then turned his attention back to me. "You okay, gorgeous?"

"I'm fine. Just checking on my artist. I actually have to—"

"I know. I just wanted to say hi. I needed to see you."

I smiled, trying hard not to let him know he was wearing me down.

"Can we talk after if you're still here?" I said before I could stop myself.

A smile crept onto his face. "What? You have time for little ole' me? Absolutely."

I shook my head. "Whatever. I'll come find you."

"Don't forget."

I looked at him one last time before disappearing into the green room. As I waited for Winter to come out of the bathroom, I sat in the chair in front of the mirror where she'd sat a few hours ago, getting her hair and makeup done. As I stared at the woman looking back at me in the mirror, I realized something. My father had replied to my question about how he was doing with how his health was, his business and ministry, but he never really said how he was doing.

I didn't want to become that person. Someone who responded based on how my business or professional life was going. I opened up my phone and decided to do something I'd never done since being in this industry. I responded to his DM.

Hey, you. I know this is weird, since I just saw you, but I figured we could start here. Your DM was cute. Very. I'm not sure what's going on, but if you can give me some time, maybe I'll say yes to a date with you. I'm going to be honest, I don't usually date within the industry, but I'm not going to front as if I don't feel the chemistry. I do. But I ask that you be patient with me. Please. Talk soon. E.

I hit send before I could change my mind, just as Winter came out of the bathroom.

"Hey, Boss Lady."

She walked over and hugged me. "This is going so much better than I thought it would. Thank you again for this opportunity."

I leaned up. "Winter, you deserve opportunities like this. You're amazing and we're going to make sure the world knows it. I promise."

She nodded, then I continued.

"Now, about this last set…"

* * *

OTHER THAN A FEW technical snafus toward the end, Winter not only wowed the crowd, but she left me and Trish with our mouths open. She went from pushing back against these new Billie Holiday meets Rachel Kerr type songs to singing them like she had written them. When I looked around the room, there were some tears, some mouths hanging open and, of course, some people just sitting in awe. This had been one of her best performances to date and I was ready to capitalize off it.

I was now driving home, listening to a sermon. I was ready to hop in the tub. One of the challenges of long days was that I didn't get to spend as much time with God as I would like throughout the day. That was why I protected my morning time so fiercely. Everyone knew not to hit me before nine, no matter what. I woke up at six and spent the first few hours of my day in prayer, worship, and reading my word. I needed it. There were times my days didn't end until nine or ten at night and I needed my spiritual vitamins.

As I pulled into my condominium's garage, my phone went off. I hadn't responded to any notifications because the two people who I would normally respond to, were with me all night. Anything else could wait until I got out of the tub. I pulled into my parking spot and turned off the car. I was pleased with how things had gone over the last few days. I even checked Winter's social media before we left Mocha Tea & Trends and she had already gained eleven thousand new followers just from today. There were clips of her performance going viral on TikTok and Instagram. We hired a videographer to take some clips for her YouTube page, but other than us getting a copy of the full performance, if you weren't there, you missed it for sure.

I hopped on the elevator and used my pass to take it up to the seventh floor. Last year, I wanted to buy a home, but thinking about the

THE ESSENCE OF HIS SOUL

responsibility that came with that was too much. I was okay with my condo until I got married and really needed a home. I wasn't sure why I was thinking of this now, but I would say I always felt like homes equated to family. I know many would disagree and I knew a lot of women who owned a home, including Trish and Winter, but I just wasn't ready. I saw my mother walk around our big home for years, often alone because my father was on the go. I didn't want that. To be honest, lately, I wasn't sure what I wanted outside of work, but I knew that needed to change.

As I ran my water for my bath and added Dr. Teal's lavender bubble foam, I poured a glass of sparkling water. I'd had enough to drink at the event and two glasses was honestly my max. As I undressed, I turned on my iPod and connected my Bluetooth. I let the sounds of Sade fill my place as I unwound from today. Once my bath was ready, I stepped inside, not caring that I'd made the water too hot. I planned on sitting here for a while.

I closed my eyes, resting my head against the neck rest of my tub. I sank into the steam and allowed the water to relax my muscles. After about twenty minutes, I decided to go ahead and check my notifications, mainly to see who was hitting me up about Winter. I knew there would be promoters hitting me up about booking her and I definitely wanted to respond to those messages, even if it was just to tell them I'd hit them back on Monday.

As I scrolled through my emails, I starred the important ones and trashed the rest. Then I headed over to social media. I opened my Instagram and checked my DMs. I had seventy-two messages, and that was just the ones in my main inbox. I probably had more in the request box. I answered a few from industry colleagues who congratulated me on the success of the show, and a few from some celebrities who had attended. I was about to close the app when I saw Shane had responded to my message.

I went to go find him before I left, but Baylock told me he left to handle something important. I didn't ask questions. As I read his message, I felt the butterflies in my stomach flutter.

Hey, gorgeous. I'm so sorry I had to leave. One of my teammates was drunk and I got a call from the bar owner to come get him. A few of us are his emergency contact. I was so irked because seeing you was the way I wanted to end my night, even if it was just for a few minutes. I appreciate you being honest with me and I have no problem being patient with you. I'm not in any rush. I think you saw my public breakup and I'm being careful with my heart the same way I want you to be careful with yours. But I do want to at least get to know you as a friend, so if you don't mind, I would love to keep DMing one another until you're comfortable giving me your number.

I was cheesing so hard reading your message. Just know that whatever is brewing between us, I'm excited to explore. Here's my number if you ever need anything, but again, take your time. SB

I read his message four times. I was halfway ready to text him and tell him to come get me, but I knew that would contradict everything I'd just said. While most athletes had a reputation, I had seen his public breakup and I had to say, I was surprised by all the details. While he hadn't spoken on it much, she had, and she admitted to cheating and breaking up with him. I wasn't saying that made him perfect, but I could tell he was a genuinely nice guy.

I locked his number in my phone, then I placed my phone down to keep from responding too quickly. Love was the last thing on my mind, prior to meeting him. Now, I was about to close my eyes and pray so I could ask God exactly what was going on with Shane Bishop because I didn't need any surprises.

Four

SHANE

"OKAY, LOVE BUG. I SEE YOU," I said, smiling at the picture Essence had sent me.

She had an event last night, so she sent me a few flicks from her phone. Two weeks had passed, and we were now texting. When she reached out via text, I was surprised. I thought it would take her a little longer since she said she wanted to take her time, but after four days of exchanging DMs, we moved to texting and talking on the phone.

So far, we'd learned a lot about each other's families and careers. I was happy to hear how she'd taken the leap of faith into music and entertainment. As for me, my team had lost our last three games and the one thing I looked forward to after every game, was hearing her voice. I used to hate when people tried to comfort me after a loss, but Essence was real when it came to that. She always encouraged me to feel whatever I wanted and to be human.

That meant a lot to me. Being a Christian could be tough when people threw scriptures at you instead of truly encouraging you when you were going through a hard time. I took game losses seriously, and not just because it meant we wouldn't make the playoffs. It was because the more losses I experienced, the more I realized I needed more than just basketball.

As I texted her back, I finished getting ready to meet with my dad. We were spending the day together since it had been at least two weeks since I'd really spent time with my old man. I noticed how distracted he was the last time we were all together as a family. I didn't want to say anything in front of my mom and sister, just in case it was a man thing he wanted to talk about. I would mention it today to see if there was something on his mind.

I threw on my sweatsuit and grabbed a cap to throw on. The real spring weather had started last week. I was finally able to just throw on a jacket if I really needed, or a thick sweatsuit that would keep me warm when the temperature dropped at night. Just when I was about to put on my sneakers, my phone went off. I thought it was my dad, but it was Essence.

I think I'm ready to take you up on your offer to hang out. What day works for you?

I almost dropped my phone, trying to respond. Smiling from ear to ear, I responded: **Let's hang out this Friday. I have the perfect spot if you're okay with hanging out indoors.**

I tapped my foot on the carpet as I waited for her to respond. I had the perfect outing planned in my mind, something I'd already been thinking about when she responded to my first DM.

I don't really like to house date, but I'm open to hearing what you have in mind.

It's more of an indoor dating facility that has bowling, a movie theater, mini golfing, zip lining, etc. But it's at a huge mansion. My friend owns it.

When the bubbles popped up, the anxiety in my chest increased.

Wow, that sounds amazing. Okay. I trust you. A little. Friday at six?

Perfect. You want to meet me there or are you okay with me picking you up?

You can pick me up. I'll be at the studio.

I waited as she sent the studio address, then I sent her back a couple of hearts. I was falling for a woman I hadn't even gone out with yet, but I didn't care. There was something special about this and I couldn't wait to find out what it was.

*   *   *

"THIS IS BEAUTIFUL. Oh my gosh. He must've worked on this for years," Essence said, as we walked through the mansion.

"He did. Once Milton knew he was retiring from basketball, he thought about how a lot of athletes and celebrities have a hard time dating because they get interrupted so much by fans wanting a picture or an autograph. He took one of his homes and turned it into this, the Date Night Mansion. You can rent it out by the hour, a half day, or a full day."

We continued walking around, stopping in the kitchen where a chef prepared the dinner I had requested.

"Wow. That's brilliant and makes a lot of sense. I wonder why I never heard of this place."

"It's pretty exclusive. There's no advertisement or website. You have to know him to book it. He gets more referrals than he can handle, but that's how he earns his business. A day in this place costs $5,000, but it's worth it for the peace and quiet, the dinner, and the fact you can have like eight dates in one day."

She looked at me. "You did not spend $5,000 on our first date?"

"I did," I said, bending down to kiss her cheek. "And I'd do it again."

She looked down at the floor. "Thank you."

"By the way, I didn't say that to brag. I just wanted you to know because I know you know people who would love this."

"Yeah. I know a lot of producers and artists who need something like this."

She grabbed my hand lightly. "So, where do we start?"

"Well, while dinner is being prepared, I figured we could relax and play some arcade games. Then, whatever you want."

She smiled. "I love that. I love letting my hair down and having fun. Plus, I'm going to kill you in Pac-Man."

She eyed the game as we entered the arcade room. There were at least fifty games in here.

"We'll see about that."

We spent the next hour playing all the old school games in the arcade, including three race car games. Then we headed out to the dining area to eat.

"Thank you, sir," I said to the chef as he placed the last dish on the table.

He bowed. "My pleasure. Ring if you need anything."

Essence looked at the herb garlic chicken smothered in a white cream sauce and smiled. "I see you listen very well."

"I do," I said, winking.

She had shared with me she only ate chicken and seafood. One thing about the menu here was that it had everything you could want, whether you were vegan or pescatarian. I reached for her hand so I could bless the food. Once I was done, I poured us both a glass of wine.

"I'll pass on the wine tonight," she said. "I'll have sparkling water, please."

"You got it, beautiful."

While we ate, I noticed how she gave me her full attention whenever I said something. I enjoyed the way she looked into my eyes as we talked.

"Is there a reason you keep doing that?"

She stopped chewing. "Doing what?"

I lightly grabbed her chin and looked into her eyes. She never broke her stare.

"That. I feel like you're piercing my soul with your eyes."

She placed her fork down, then looked at me, allowing our eyes to lock again. "I believe when you look into someone's eyes with that kind of intensity, you can see into their souls."

"Interesting. They do say the eyes are the windows to the soul."

She sat back against the chair. "They are. I can tell when someone is lying to me or when they're not giving me all the details just by looking into their eyes, and I don't even have to look that long."

I nodded in understanding. "I like looking people in their eyes, so they know I mean what I'm saying, and I like to know they mean what they're saying."

"Exactly."

We continued making small talk as we ate. When we were done, I gave her a tour of the rest of the mansion. I knew there was no way we would get through it all in one day, but I at least wanted her to see the options we had whenever we came here. Our next stop was the skating room. I hadn't skated in years, but I knew she loved it, so I was willing to do it for her.

"Okay, Mr. Ball Player. Let's see what you got," she said, lacing up her skates and gliding backward onto the floor.

"So, you showin' off?"

I stood up, wobbling a few times, but got on the floor. She was still skating backward, looking at me as she did. I enjoyed the view. Her hair blew lightly as she skated. Her legs glided effortlessly as she became one with the music. I smiled as she sped up a little, then slowed back down so I could catch up to her.

"Give me your hand," she said.

"Uh-uh. I like the speed I'm going, thank you very much."

Giggling, she slowed until she was right next to me, then she grabbed both of my hands so we were facing one another. She moved her legs and told me to follow her. It took a few minutes, but I finally got the hang of it, and while I skated frontward, she skated backward. We were in sync with one another. She wasn't going too fast and I had found a pretty good rhythm.

After about ten minutes of us skating like that, she turned around so that her back was now to me. She placed my hands on her waist and we skated like that for another few minutes.

For the next hour, we tried different positions, with her making sure I was comfortable with each before she showed me her moves. I was having a blast. I wouldn't say I was a pro, but I wasn't as bad as I thought I would be on skates. After another hour, we made our way off the floor and plopped down on the bench.

"That was too much fun," she said, catching her breath. "That was also a good workout."

I chuckled. "Now, that's the truth. My legs are burning."

"Oh, please. You barely moved them," she teased.

I pushed her playfully, then helped her take her skates off.

"Are you enjoying our first official date?" I asked.

She nodded. "I love this. It's like Dave & Buster's on steroids, except great privacy, and better food." She looked at me. "But I'm also enjoying your company. Our virtual dates have been nice, but this is everything."

"Yeah. Once the season slows down, we can hang out more, but to your point, tonight has been something else. I usually like chilling, but doing stuff like this with you is pretty cool."

Smiling, she brushed some of her hair behind her ear. "So, what's next?"

I took a few deep breaths. "Well, I figured we could watch a movie and then, call it a night. I want to get you back to the studio at a decent hour."

She looked at her watch. "It's only eight. We can go until ten."

I nodded. "Okay. Let's go then."

I grabbed her hand as we headed out of the skating area to the movie theater.

"So, what are we watching?"

"You said you love thrillers and action movies, so I thought we could enjoy the latest *Equalizer*."

"Oh, I'm so ready. Let's do it."

"You want a snack?" I asked as we entered the theater section.

"Your friend must be a billionaire off this place. He thought of everything."

I laughed. "He did."

"I'm okay for now. Dinner has me full."

We entered the theater room.

"After you," I said, as she chose seats in the middle.

I noticed how comfortable she appeared to be. That was my biggest goal throughout the night: to make her comfortable. I knew she wasn't the type to listen to what everyone else had to say, but everyone had their thoughts about basketball players. I couldn't blame them, especially when I thought about some of my own teammates. She looked over at me.

"Thank you," she said, as the lights grew dimmer.

"For what?"

"Making me comfortable. I appreciate that."

I wasn't sure if she had read my mind or her discernment was just that powerful, but either way, I felt like I was winning.

"Anytime, beautiful. Anytime."

***

I COULDN'T STOP GRINNING. Tonight went way better than I expected. I knew Essence was a down-to-earth woman, but she really let her hair down. Even when I dropped her back off at the studio so she could get her car, she was dancing and singing as she got out of my truck and made her way over to her car. She had me doubled over, laughing. That was the one thing I noticed about her when we first started texting.

She was free. Most people I came across in the entertainment business were always weighed down by something, whether it was their career, the blogs and rumors or just their own expectations of themselves. You could see the heaviness on them and around them. With Essence, she was carefree. I knew she had some things that stressed her out about her career, but she definitely wore her frustrations with grace. I'd never heard her complain one time.

I walked into my home and threw my jacket on the couch. I knew I wouldn't let it stay there. I was a sucker for a neat place, especially where I rested my head, but I was still in a playful mood. I decided to call Essence. She was supposed to call me when she made it home, but I wanted to get on her nerves now.

"I'm not home yet," she said, as soon as she answered. "I need another ten minutes."

"I know you're not. I just wanted to hear your voice."

I knew I was falling hard and fast, but honestly, I liked it. I never tried to be someone I wasn't. Most of the guys I knew tried to be players and they wanted to prove they were too tough for love, but I wasn't like that. I didn't want to be.

"Well, you heard it. Now, let me call you when I get in. I hate talking and driving."

Laughing, I gave in. "Okay. Okay."

Neither one of us hung up.

"You didn't hang up," I teased.

"You hang up first," she said. "You called me."

"Okay. We'll both hang up on three."

Her high-pitched laughter came through the phone. "What are we, three? Bye, boy."

When I heard the click, I smiled. She was definitely getting to me. I noticed it was reciprocated, though. She called me as much as I called her and we both seemed to let our guards down at the same pace.

I walked over to the couch and sat down. Throwing my legs up, I opened the Instagram app and started scrolling through my timeline. I tried not to spend too much time on this thing, but it got hard when I didn't have a game. It was hard reading the negative comments about our team.

We definitely got a lot of love, but those negative comments felt like a bunch of bee stings. I was about to close out the app when I saw the airplane in the corner. I barely checked my DMs now that Essence and I were connected via phone. Curiosity got the best of me and I opened it. My mouth fell open when I saw the message. What did she want?

Hey, stranger. Long time no talk to. It's been forever since we last talked. I know you're probably wondering what I want, but I just wanted to see if you would like to meet up for coffee. Since you own the hottest latte spot in town, I can meet you there. Just let me know when.

I almost cursed when I was done reading. A lot had transpired in Rayna's life since she publicly humiliated me, including losing her baby to a miscarriage and the guy she cheated on me with leaving her for a white woman. The last year of my life had been peaceful and I wasn't about to disturb that peace for anybody. I went to her page, hit the block button, then deleted the message. The past was the past.

Five

ESSENCE

SPRUCE Street Harbor Park was packed. I knew it would be. It was a beautiful Saturday in April and people were excited to get out and have a good time. We'd had a pretty rough winter here, so it was no surprise we'd already gotten stopped three times as people asked for Shane's autograph or a picture. By the fourth interruption, he politely declined and pulled me closer to him.

"Sorry about that," he said.

"No worries. I'm used to this," I said. "Believe it or not, everybody wants a picture with Bishop and First Lady Taylor."

We walked hand in hand to the cotton candy station.

"I know we've talked about it, but I don't think you ever really shared how it made you feel to grow up in the spotlight like that."

Once we arrived, he ordered a large cotton candy for us to share.

"Hey, man. This one's on the house. Thanks for how you hold the city down," the man who took our order said.

"Aww, man, I can't do that. It's just cotton candy. Let me pay."

"No, really. It's all good."

Shane looked around. "Okay. What if I give you a hundred bucks and that covers whoever comes by for the next hour or so? Deal?"

The guy grinned. "Sure. Thanks so much. And I know you'll win the next few games. I can feel it."

While he continued chatting with the man, I couldn't help but admire how he was with everyone we'd connected with here. Even when he declined the last person, he was so gentle about it, the young guy couldn't help but smile, anyway. Once he grabbed our cotton candy, we walked over to the benches that were a few feet away and sat down. He waved at a few people who called his name, then turned his attention back to me.

"Now, do you see why I would pay $5,000 a day just to spend time with you?"

Laughing, I nodded. "I do. I really get it, but if you rented that place for like a week or something, your friend needs to give you some type of lifetime membership."

He looked at me. "That's not a bad idea. I'm going to ask him about it."

"Honestly, do you think that's why you haven't found someone to settle down with yet?"

He turned to face me. "What do you mean?"

I collected my thoughts, then spoke. "One of the things I noticed about my mother is that she always seemed sad whenever my father was gone for a long period of time. I asked her about it once and she shared with me how difficult it can be to have to lend your spouse out to everyone else because you understand their calling and don't want to be selfish, but you also don't want them to forget you."

"She had a lot of missed anniversaries and birthdays. I'm just wondering if that plays a role in you not settling down yet. I know you were engaged, but do you think she was afraid of all it would require to be with you?"

He put another piece of cotton candy into his mouth, then handed it to me. I took a few pieces off and closed my eyes as it melted in my mouth.

"I never thought about that. It's interesting because, even in therapy, I think the focus for me was healing from the public heartbreak and humiliation rather than trying to understand why she left or handled things the way she did."

THE ESSENCE OF HIS SOUL

I brushed a few pieces of lint off his shirt. "Now, wait. I'm not giving this girl a pass because she was dead wrong. But even before her, have you ever considered the challenges of settling down with an athlete or someone that's a celebrity?"

I could tell by the look on his face that it was something he hadn't really thought about. He seemed perplexed.

"To be honest, how about I ask you that same question, but reframe it? How would you handle being with someone like me? There's a reason we're both here with each other, right? We want to see where this goes."

I leaned against him as he placed his arm around my shoulder. "Well, I can say part of me is a little nervous about it because I did see my mother get put on the back burner a lot, and you're way more popular than my dad."

We shared a laugh.

"But I watched how you handled today. You listened when I told you I wanted to come here, and you made it happen. You didn't bring any bodyguards, you just wanted to have a regular day out. You've been balancing acknowledging your fans and making me feel seen pretty well. I'm just wondering how long it will last."

He looked at me. "As long as we want it to."

"Is it really that easy?"

He stood up. "Come on. Follow me."

He grabbed my hand as I threw away the last bit of cotton candy. We walked over to the photo booth and I watched as he placed three dollars in the machine, then pulled me inside. We took a bunch of photos, as many as the two-minute timer would let us take, then fell out of the booth, laughing. As we waited for them to print, he brushed my hair out of my face.

"That was fun," I said softly.

"Sometimes I don't like to think about why stuff doesn't work. I just want to show you it can."

I cocked my head to the side. He shrugged.

"You're not asking anything a man shouldn't be able to answer. I just think I need time to give you a proper answer."

The pictures came out of the machine just when I was about to respond. They were attached in fours, so there were three sets. I grabbed them before he could and almost dropped them from laughing so hard. From the first picture to the last, there were funny faces, shocking reactions and weird facial expressions. I didn't think there was a normal picture in the bunch where we simply smiled. He finally snatched one set out of my hand.

"Please don't post these on social media."

"Oh, I'm way ahead of you," I teased.

As we continued joking, I felt a few drops of water on my arm. At first, I thought the weatherman had lied and it was rain, but when I looked to my right, I realized we were close to the water. There were a few people doing a rowing competition and a few off to the side, fishing.

"I would love to get on the boats," I said, grabbing his hand. "I think the line starts over there, though they'll probably let you go in front."

I tried to pull him ahead, but he wouldn't budge. I turned around.

"What's wrong?"

He stared out at the water with a blank expression on his face.

"Uh, earth to Shane. You okay?"

I saw him swallow. His eyes finally landed back on me.

"I don't do water. Maybe we can head over to the Ping-Pong table and play a few games."

He was already walking in the opposite direction before I could respond. I wasn't pressed to go on the boat ride, but his reaction was definitely weird. I was quiet as I caught up to him. He reached back and grabbed my hand and I felt myself relaxing again.

"You okay?"

"I'm fine," he responded, jaws clenched.

I decided it was best to be quiet and to follow his lead. As type A as I could be, I could tell this wasn't personal. I saw the sadness in his eyes as he looked out at the water. If I was honest, I think I could even see a little fear. One thing my father taught me, was how to read people's body language and what their eyes said before they even spoke a word.

We continued walking, and as we moved through the crowd, my mind drifted back to the last few weeks. This was only our second in-person date, but we talked on the phone every day, texting throughout the day, and we'd had a bunch of virtual dates. I was opening up in ways I hadn't expected, and now, I felt like he was shutting down. My discernment was pretty strong, but I couldn't put my finger on this one. I guess I would have to wait until he was ready to open up about it.

He slowed down a little, which I was grateful for. While I had on a cute pair of wedge sandals that had a low heel, his long legs definitely made me have to walk fast to keep up.

"Sorry about that," he said, slowing his pace even more. "I just had to get away from there."

I remained quiet, scared that if I stepped on the landmine, it would certainly go off.

"Why don't we lay down in the hammocks over there?" he asked. "If you're comfortable with that."

I nodded. He looked at me, then looked away. We found an empty hammock and he got in first, then I laid down next to him. I waited for him to speak, but when he didn't, I started talking about a new artist Trish and I had signed. I was trying to find the balance we had a few minutes ago, at the picture booth, but he was giving me one-word answers and smiling at me weakly as I talked. Finally, he leaned up.

"Is it okay if we get out of here?"

I stroked the side of his face. "Of course."

Back in his truck, he started the engine. As he took the car out of park, he gripped the steering wheel tightly.

"My brother drowned when he was six," he blurted out.

I swallowed, not knowing at all what to say to that. Until now, whenever we talked about our families, I'd never even heard about a brother. I waited for him to keep going, but there was nothing. Silence fell over us as I reached for his hand. He turned slightly to me. The glassiness in his eyes was evident against the sunrays that forced their way into his truck.

"It's okay if you don't want to talk about it," I said.

He shook his head. "I don't, but... You have to know. It's the only way you can understand certain parts of me."

I took a deep breath, bracing myself for the story.

"It was my fault," he said, in a much lower tone. "Pool accident."

I blinked a few times. I definitely wasn't expecting that.

"I was eight at the time and our parents were preparing sandwiches and snacks for us to enjoy as a family out back by our pool. We were like one of the only families in the neighborhood with a pool." He smirked. "At the time, I thought we were the luckiest family ever. Sahana was inside with our parents, but Samuel and I were doing cannonballs in the pool."

He stopped and shifted in his seat. He closed his eyes. "The pool only went up to five feet. We all had swimming lessons. There was no reason to think we wouldn't be okay. But Samuel went too far. He wanted to try a cannonball on the five feet side, and I kept telling him not to, or to at least wait until our parents were back outside with us, but Samuel had to prove himself that he could do it. So, he did."

The tears rolled slowly down his face. This was the first time I'd ever seen him this vulnerable and, to be honest, I wasn't sure what to do other than give his hand a little squeeze every few minutes.

"When he didn't come back up to the surface automatically, I knew something was wrong. I thought he was playing around at first, but then I saw the blood. I ran over, but I was too scared to jump in. I went back around to the three feet side and swam over to him. I tried moving his body with my arms when I reached him, but I was starting to go under. I was trying to tread water and save him at the same time."

His phone buzzed. He looked at his dashboard to see who was calling. I was kind of grateful for the break. This story was heavy.

"I'll call her back," he said, staring straight ahead. "Funny that Sahana would call right now."

He rubbed his goatee a few times, then continued. "Finally, I got out of the pool and ran inside to tell our parents. I remember my mom dropping the pitcher of lemonade and glass shattering everywhere. My father was right behind her. They got him out, but it was too late. He was blue, his nose was bleeding, and his chest wasn't moving. They tried CPR, but..."

I wiped at his face as I slid closer to him. I think I'd seen my father cry all of two times in my life and I could honestly count on both hands how many times my mother had cried. I grappled for words, but as he grabbed me around the waist and pulled me closer to him, I realized I didn't need to say anything. I just needed to be. Be here in the moment with him.

* * *

AS I ENTERED MY CONDO, I threw my shoes off and headed to the bathroom. I was too exhausted to take a bath, so I was just going to take a quick shower and decompress. As I turned the water on, I thought about the last time I'd been close enough to someone who shared their deepest secrets with me. My ex, Dixon, and I had shared some deep, intimate moments, but nothing like this. In fact, that was why we broke up, because he shared one of those moments with the wrong person and my family's business became public overnight. Shane was opening up to me quicker than I expected, but when I thought back to our phone conversations, it made sense.

We would talk throughout the day, at least five times a day. We sent voice memos back and forth and we texted all the time. In the last six weeks, we had quickly become like best friends. We honestly slid into the dating part easily because of the bond we shared. If I was honest, I realized one of the reasons I didn't know what to say when he was talking was because I didn't have experience in dealing with the broken pieces of a man.

This was the kind of thing people said you should deal with in therapy. Dixon would laugh if I even mentioned the idea of therapy. My biggest struggle now was making sure I was the woman I needed to be to handle Shane's broken pieces. Don't get it twisted, I wasn't running. In fact, I prayed over him before he dropped me off. Then I prayed again as I rode the elevator up to my floor. I prayed God would equip me to love this man right.

"God, is this love?" I asked out loud.

I wasn't sure what we would call it yet, but I knew God knew what it was. When we first connected, I was adamant I didn't even want to deal with a basketball player. Now, I was asking God to show me how to handle his heart right. If this wasn't love, I wasn't sure what was. We were still going slow and he was being patient, but could I really control the rhythm of my heart when I was with him? Did I even want to?

Just when I was about to step into the shower, my phone went off. I hoped it was him, although I told him to relax and give me a call only when he was up to it. I grabbed my phone.

"What the hell?" I said as I read the text.

Clayton.

I'd forgotten all about the fact my father had given him my number. When I didn't hear from him that night, I dismissed it and thanked God he hadn't called. But as I read his text, I understood why.

Hey, beautiful. It's been forever. I'm sorry for just reaching out. I was on a combo business and mission trip in Mexico and just got back a few days ago. I've been dying to talk to you. Let's do dinner tomorrow night. Oh, and I love your hair. Yes, I've been stalking your Instagram.

I wasn't sure whether to throw up or throw my phone. It was the audacity that he felt like I had to do dinner with him. Thank God, Shane had a game tomorrow night. It was actually the game that would decide if they would at least be in the playoffs. If they lost, this was it. But even if I had nothing to do, the answer would be no. Instead of responding, I decided to text Shane.

Hey, handsome. I just wanted to send you some love before I hopped in the shower. I know opening up like that wasn't easy, but I'm glad you feel safe with me. Let me know how I can be there for you. E

I placed my phone down, then jumped in the shower. As I washed the heaviness of the day off me, I thought about Shane. I smiled as his face came to my mind. I saw him licking his lips a million times in between every word. Laughing, I squeezed more soap on my washcloth and continued washing. I stopped smiling when I realized there was a talk we definitely needed to have before we went any further. It was actually one of the reasons I hadn't dated in two years. I was abstinent and I planned on keeping it that way until my wedding night. I was just hoping Mr. Shane Bishop was cool with that.

Six

SHANE

I LOOKED AT THE SCOREBOARD, thinking if I could just blink a few more times, the number would change and I could attempt the shot again, but it didn't. *Ninety-two to eighty-nine.* If I would've made the last three-pointer, we would've at least gone into overtime. Our season was over.

I tried to swallow the lump in my throat, but I couldn't even breathe. The fact we still had a chance to make it and we'd blown it caused my chest to tighten. I saw Kevell out of the corner of my eye. He walked over to me. I felt his hand on my back.

"Yo, bro. We had a good season. I know it hurts, but we did our best," he said, his voice cracking.

I looked at him and grabbed him in a hug. Some people may not understand, but the tears that fell from our eyes were tears we'd been holding in all season long. We took every win and loss personal, but tonight was the blow that knocked the wind out of us. The Philadelphia Panthers hadn't been to the playoffs since the first year I joined the team, which was four years ago. Each year, I promised the city a championship and each year, I'd failed them.

I know I shouldn't be carrying the weight of it all on my own, but I was the star player, the point guard. The leading scorer. How could I not think like that?

More teammates came over as we hugged it out. Finally, we made our way over to the other team to congratulate them. I was close to two of the players on the other team and when they hugged me, they actually shared in my sorrow, which made it worse.

As I walked over to the bench, the crowd did something I wasn't expecting. Losing at home was a hard pill to swallow, but I watched as, one by one, everyone stood up and started clapping. The arena shook as they stomped the floor and chanted my name. I felt the floor vibrating under my feet. The sound grew louder and that made my tears flow harder. I knew our fans wouldn't let us down. That was one of the reasons I traded to Philadelphia. The loyalty was insane. I grabbed a towel and wiped my face. Then I walked over to the announcer's stand and grabbed a mic.

"Thank you. Thank you," I said, clearing my throat. "You guys are the best. I mean, the absolute best. From your social media support, to when you see us out and about with our families, to right now in this moment. We adore you all. This season has been long and rough, but we carried it as a team. I'm not making you guys any more promises."

The arena erupted with laughter.

"But I will say this. We won't stop playing hard for you. Thank you for your love and support."

I handed the mic back to the announcer, then waved at the crowd as we headed toward the locker room. I slapped the hands that stuck out from the sides as I headed back. I even stopped and took a few pictures with some of the younger fans. I wasn't really in the mood, but it came with the game.

As I got closer to the locker room, security and other staff members clapped and saluted me and the rest of the team. I was trying my hardest not to be a big crybaby, but who could blame me?

I bent down to take another quick picture, then stood up. When my eyes landed on her, I almost ran over to her. I kept my composure as I made my way over to her. Though I hated she saw me lose, I was happy I'd invited her to my final game of the season. She opened her arms and I fell into them.

"Hey, Baby Girl," I whispered in her ear.

"Hey, love. I'm sorry you guys didn't win."

I pulled back slightly. "It's okay. Seeing you makes me feel better."

"That last attempt was epic. I caught it on camera. I know you probably didn't see what most of us saw because you missed, but to me, that was the greatest play of the game."

I winked, then pulled her closer to me as we walked to the locker room door.

"I have to shower and get dressed. Then you know there'll be a huge press conference. The wives and girlfriends usually wait out there or in the room right next door."

She shrugged. "I'll wait wherever you need me to. I told you we were going to celebrate, regardless. My treat."

I forced a smile. "Okay."

I leaned down and kissed her. It was the first time I had pecked her on the mouth. She didn't resist. "I know I'm funky. Give me an hour."

She wrinkled her nose. "I'll give you two," she said, exiting the area.

Laughing, I walked into the locker room and walked over to my hub, and fell on my knees. The weight of this season came crashing down on me as I cried one last time.

*　*　*

"THESE ARE BEAUTIFUL, BABE," she said, touching the edge of the painting that was in my office.

While we'd been dating for a little over a month, this was her first time getting a full tour of my place. She'd been to my place only once before, since we spent most of our time dating out, and when we did do indoors, we either did the mansion or her place to make her feel comfortable.

"I got that painting the day after I signed to Philadelphia. I wanted something that spoke to how I felt."

She eyed it closely, then touched it lightly with the tips of her fingers. "The detail is crazy. This man is clearly happy about something. I love the way the artist captured his dual emotions." She looked at me. "So, you were happy and scared?"

I nodded. I gulped the water I was drinking. Since we'd gotten back to my place an hour ago, I'd been drinking water non-stop. My mouth was dry, and I knew it had to do with all the crying I'd done.

"Signing to Philadelphia was major for me. I'm from New Jersey, so naturally, everyone thought I'd sign with the Nets. But I knew Philadelphia was going to be my home."

She walked closer to me. "How? I mean, I love my city, but what made you fall in love with it?"

I placed my glass down on the edge of my desk. Grabbing her hand, I led her into another room—my prayer room. My parents had been the only people up here, but I wanted her to see it. Most of my decisions were made in this place.

"I thought I was the only one who had a full room dedicated to prayer," she said.

"I think most PKs know the deal," I joked. "Honestly, it's the reason I wanted a three-bedroom condo. To answer your question, this is why I chose Philadelphia after getting cut from the Clippers. God spoke to me about Philly long before I graduated from college. I knew I wanted to do the full four years, no matter who tried to draft me."

She raised an eyebrow. "Really? I mean, I knew you finished, but I didn't know it was because you chose to. I thought nobody wanted you."

I picked up the plush dice that was on my desk and threw it at her. She laughed as she swatted it away from her.

"You got jokes? Can you remember that I'm still hurting after tonight's game?"

She blew me a kiss. "I'm sorry, baby."

She reached out her arms and I fell into her embrace. Closing my eyes, I stayed there for a minute before pulling away.

"When I tell you God has been guiding my career since day one, I'm not lying. I knew when I graduated from high school, God wanted me to finish school. I wrote it down in my prayer journal and promised God I wouldn't stray from His plan."

"That had to be hard."

"Harder than losing tonight's game."

I continued telling her about my journey throughout college, highlighting how even when a few teams wanted to draft me during my sophomore and junior years, my father would remind me of my promise to God and I held out. I turned down three multi-million-dollar contracts throughout college just to keep my word. I told her about my first two years in the NBA playing for the Clippers, who had reached out the year after I graduated. But God allowed me to be cut from the team after almost three years and I ended up in Philly, exactly where He had told me in the beginning.

"That's why I believe your word is all you have. Nobody but God and my dad would know if I broke my promise, but if you break your word to God, are you any good to anyone?"

"You know what's so funny?" she asked as we headed out of the prayer room and back to the kitchen. I noticed she grabbed my empty glass as we were leaving.

"What?"

"When we first met at the coffee shop, I remember saying to myself how there was such a peace about you I couldn't explain. I felt it."

My eyes landed on her beautiful, bronze skin as she poured me another glass of water, adding a lemon to it. Her Cuban features stood out tonight, more than they ever had before. I knew women used bronzer for their skin sometimes, but Essence's skin was naturally bronzy. When she handed me the glass, I smiled. She looked into my eyes as I brushed her hair out of her face.

"It looks like your hair is growing back faster than you wanted," I said.

"I know. That's why I don't like cutting it. It just grows right back."

I took a few gulps of the water, then put the glass down. Wiping my hands on my pants, I lightly grabbed her face as she moved closer to me.

"May I?"

She nodded.

This time, I kissed her for real. She let my tongue meet hers. As our bodies leaned into one another, I took my time tasting her lips, but made sure to release before either of us got too excited.

"Wow," she whispered.

I turned her toward the living room, then walked beside her closely as I led us into the living room. As we sat on the couch, she kicked her legs up and threw them on my lap.

"I have a question," she said, breaking me out of my thoughts.

"Shoot, gorgeous."

"Do you think the way you dealt with waiting on God to bring this promise to pass explains why you're so patient with everything else?"

I wasn't expecting that. It was actually a great question.

"You know what's so funny, I think it did. When I signed to the Clippers, I kept asking God what about Philadelphia, but He confirmed Los Angeles so many times. I realized that what I learned playing for the Clippers actually prepared me to be the star player for Philly."

She nodded.

"Enough about me, Baby Girl. Tell me more about your world. What are your dreams?"

She leaned back deeper into the pillows that were behind her. "I've always wanted to win the ASCAP Writer of the Year award, and I've always wanted to produce an entire album on my own. Those are my goals for this year."

"That's big. What does it take to do either of those things?" I asked, grabbing her feet and massaging them. She closed her eyes and laid her head back.

"If you don't stop, I'll be over here every day for one of these."

After a few minutes of me massaging, she responded. "Well, I've written thirty-two songs over the course of my career, mainly R&B and soul. I have a few pop hits in there, but the focus has always been R&B. To be honest, this industry is so saturated, I'm not sure anymore what the criteria is, but I just know I'm always writing and selling my songs." She took a deep breath. "As far as the other goal, well, this industry thrives off collabs. I love working with Dev Hits, Mike Jay, and all the other major producers that make this business worth working in. It takes a lot to produce an album and it can be done, but because I also manage, I don't have the time."

I listened intently as she shared her process for how she came up with her songs, how she and Trish decided an artist was worth signing, and how she got to work with people she was always inspired by. I almost choked when she told me how much she made just for one song.

THE ESSENCE OF HIS SOUL

I knew songwriters and producers made good money, but hearing it out loud was intriguing. Now I understood why most of my teammates wanted to be rappers at some point. I chuckled.

"What?"

"I was just thinking about how most of my teammates swear they want to put out at least one rap album in their career."

She laughed. "Yeah. That's definitely funny. Everybody wants to be a rapper or break into the music business somehow."

I grabbed her hand. "I'm proud of you. The way you just broke all of that down made me respect what you do even more. You're not just a producer or songwriter. You're a mogul. Maybe your award is in that."

She smiled weakly. "That was sweet. To be clear, I'm not pressed for the award. I know I'm blessed. I think it's just something to aim for."

We spent a few more minutes talking about our careers, with me trying not to talk too much about tonight's loss. The press conference had been grueling enough. I had to admit, I was glad the season was over. Essence and I could spend more time together and I could figure out what life had for me outside of basketball.

"You want some cookies and cream ice cream?" I asked.

"That sounds good. I think we earned dessert since we had salmon salads for dinner."

I got up and headed to the kitchen. I hadn't been in the mood to eat dessert in the restaurant. I made sure we had a private area so we could enjoy the meal in private, but I didn't want to stay too long.

I dipped out two bowls of ice cream, then headed back to the living room.

"Thank you, handsome."

I couldn't help but blush a little when she called me that. We dug into our ice cream. Her phone went off. As she checked it, I noticed how quickly her smile faded. She turned the phone over and placed it on the coffee table. I looked at her, searching for answers.

"My father. Nothing major."

I noticed that whenever she brought him up, she kept it brief and barely said much about him. I knew he was overbearing, but that was it. I never pushed the issue, especially since we both still had a lot to learn about each other's families.

"So, what else does that pretty brain of yours think about?"

She looked up at the ceiling, then placed her spoon back in the bowl. "I used to have this blog called The Essentials of Life. I wrote every day – articles on life, faith, the business, love, everything. It was something I really enjoyed and lately, I've been thinking about bringing it back."

"Judging by the way your eyes lit up and how you just said all of that in one breath, I think you should."

She giggled. "You think so? I don't know. It was just for fun. Nothing major, although I could've monetized it. I had about two thousand followers."

"Anything that makes you feel like this, all bubbly and excited, you should focus on. Even if it's just for fun. Everything doesn't have to be about money."

She ate a spoonful of her ice cream. "You make me bubbly and excited."

My eyes widened. "So, are you saying you tryna focus on me?"

She bit her bottom lip. "Well, I have to see if I can fit you into my schedule, but I think I can make something work."

I chuckled, then pulled her closer to me. I fed her some of my ice cream, then grabbed both of our bowls and placed them on the coffee table.

"I'm willing to wait until you figure it out."

I watched as her eyes landed on her phone, then back on me. "You won't have to wait long."

Our lips met again, this time, the taste of cookies and sweet vanilla exploded in my mouth as our tongues met. It was the perfect sweet ending to a bittersweet day.

Seven

ESSENCE

"SO, we're all set on signing her?" I asked Trish.

We were full swing into our second quarter goals, and things were moving along pretty well. It was about to be the end of April and we wanted to sign one last artist so we could balance out our performance schedule and earn on that side of the business.

"Yes. I think Remi is perfect for what we're looking for. She has that Neo-soul vibe, and her looks are very eclectic. I love her cheekbones."

I looked at Trish and laughed. "I knew you would love those cheekbones," I teased.

Trish was half-African and Cuban and her cheekbones were the envy of plenty of models and women who paid for them in our industry.

"You know I'm a sucker for a dope headshot," she said, laughing. "But honestly, her numbers are amazing, she works her butt off and, from what her last manager said, she's only struggling to get signed because she won't take off her clothes. Gotta respect that."

I nodded. "That's actually one of the reasons I was happy to meet with her. She definitely makes me feel good about scheduling her for some benefit concerts or high school talks where she can motivate some of the youth."

Trish nodded. "I love it. I guess all that's left to do is send her lawyer the ninety-day trial period contract and take it from there."

I grinned. This would conclude Taylor Made Music Group's roster for the rest of the year. After signing Remi, we would have four artists: Winter Daze, May Reed, Remi and the only man, Coffee Tan. We also had one producer signed to us, Majestic Hits, so with five people, we would have our work cut out for us. We made all new artists sign a ninety-day trial period contract just to give both parties a chance to see if it was a good fit. So far, everyone passed our ninety-day trial.

"I'll email it over before I head out to lunch since I have a date," Trish said.

I spun my chair around and slapped her thigh. "Uh-uh. Is that why you ditched me last night? Shane kept asking why you didn't come to the game."

She stuck her tongue out at me. "For your information, I canceled because my sister showed up at my house after another fight with her boyfriend. I just didn't feel like talking about it."

I got serious. "I'm sorry, sis. She's still with him?"

"Girl, I would be surprised if they ever break up, but I had to put my boundaries up last night. Enough is enough. I'm tired of carrying her."

I nodded in understanding. While I was an only child, my parents had siblings who thought, just because they had money and were the responsible ones, they had to take care of their problems.

"Anyway," she continued, "I met Maurice at Mocha Tea & Trends. They had their April mixer last weekend, but you were hanging with Shane. I went just to kind of network, especially with the success we had when Winter performed. He was there."

"Nice. So, are you feeling where it's going?"

She crossed her legs. "Is it weird to fall quickly for someone when you don't even have time to date?"

I clapped my hands. "Listen, Honey. You're preaching to the choir. I thought between both of our busy schedules, we would barely be able to build a connection. Lies, girl. All lies. I've never felt so connected to someone in my life."

She raised an eyebrow. "Dixon?"

I flagged her off. "That was a make-believe connection compared to this. I'm not trying to dismiss our good times, but the first day I met Shane, there was a peace I can't describe. You know how I am about people's character."

She nodded. "I think that's what I like about Maurice. We've been out three times and the way he carries himself and how he handles people is different. I always say in this business, the way people treat those who can't do anything for them speaks volumes. But I watched someone disrespect him—"

"Wait... what?"

"It was someone drunk. Nothing major. But even the way he handled that, it was like, were you one of the twelve disciples or something?"

"Well, that means he was John because Peter was cutting ears."

We shared a laugh.

"Listen, sis, take your time and go at your own pace, but don't run from it. You know I ain't the mushy type and Shane has me doing and saying things after five weeks that I wouldn't normally say in six months."

"Wait... doing?"

I stood up, giving her a playful push. "Oh girl, please. This thing is locked until I hear 'I do'. As hard as it is, and as hard as these last two years have been, I don't care how good you treat me. Without a covenant, she ain't coming out to play."

We grabbed our bags as we shared another laugh. I looked around our office and smiled. Taking in the purple and gold décor, I had to say I was beaming, thinking about what we'd built.

"We've done good for ourselves, Trish," I said. "By the grace of God, we've built something solid here. Maybe it's time we focus on our hearts."

She gave me a high-five. "I second that. Because if I feel like this after three dates, he may be the one."

As we rode the elevator down, I thought about what I'd told her. I was going with the flow when it came to Shane. Trish and I had been so focused for the last few years. Dixon was the person I'd let distract me, but even then, he knew business came first. Now, as we parted ways, heading to our separate cars, I realized love was definitely calling my name, and this time, I was willing to answer.

* * *

"YOU SHOULD'VE REPLIED to my text," my father said, his voice bellowing over the blender. He was making us his famous peanut butter and banana smoothie.

I rolled my eyes upward as he handed me mine. Cocking my head to the side, I smiled.

"There's nothing funny, Essence. You're becoming more and more disrespectful by the day. It's probably that demonic industry you're in."

I tried to hold it in, but I couldn't. I bust out laughing. "Dad, are you serious?"

He drank some of his smoothie. "I'm dead serious."

I gasped. "Did you just say dead? I thought life and death was in the power of the tongue. Shouldn't you be careful about saying 'dead serious'?"

He scowled. I knew I was being difficult, but I was going to make him pay for sending me that text.

"I don't get it. Clayton is a great guy. He's respectful, comes from a great family and he doesn't have any children or drama." He checked his phone. "I bet you can't say that about half the men who approach you in Hollywood."

I took a few sips of my smoothie as I picked up my phone. I still hadn't told my parents I was seeing Shane. It wasn't because I was afraid, I just wanted to make sure what we had was solid first. I'd been praying about it and God continued to confirm he was someone I could trust.

"I'm dating someone," I blurted. I wanted to wait, but as I held my phone in my hand, re-reading my father's last text, I couldn't help it.

I'm having dinner with Clayton and his father in an hour. You need to get here as soon as possible. Even if you can make dessert, that's still enough time for you guys to talk and have a moment.

I shook my head as I placed my phone back down.

"Dating who? Your mother didn't say anything to me about you dating someone."

That's because I didn't tell her, I thought. "I'll let you guys know when I'm ready, but for now, Clayton isn't an option."

My father stood up. "You don't even know if this will work out."

I finished my smoothie, then stood up. "Dad, Clayton will never be an option, even if I'm the last single woman on earth and he's the last single man."

My father's jaw clenched. Good. Now he understood how I felt last night. To be honest, if my parents read blogs and entertainment news, they would've seen a few pictures of Shane and me out together. Most of them were of our backs or our sides, so nobody could officially make out my face, but they knew it was him for sure. Rumors were swirling about the new beauty he had on his arm. I wasn't worried, though. We had both agreed to stay private until we were ready.

"You act like he's horrible."

My mother sauntered into the kitchen, kissing my cheek lightly. "Honey, please lay off our baby girl."

I swirled around, my mouth hanging open. Melissa Taylor had never told my dad to get off my back, especially when it came to finding a suitor for his only daughter.

"Mom, are you feeling okay?" I asked, touching her forehead as she poured herself a cup of tea.

She frowned, confusion settling onto her face. I tried to hide my smile, but I was having too much fun messing with my parents.

"I'm fine, Honey," she responded, moving toward my father. "We have a meeting at two with Sandy and the Higgins."

"What's going on with them?" I asked, remembering how many years Sandy and her family had been faithful to my parents' church.

My father grunted. "You would know that if you took the position at the church that was waiting for you."

My mother rolled her eyes. She was surprising me by the second, but I remained quiet. "Sandy's granddaughter was arrested, and they weren't able to bail her out. We're trying to see how we can help."

"Wait, are you talking about Lyric? What happened?"

I felt concern setting in. Lyric was only sixteen and she could sing her behind off. I'd consider signing her when she turned eighteen, but my father would never forgive me for turning a church girl into a Hollywood songstress.

"It's a long story, dear," my mother continued. "We'll talk about it later." She turned to my father. "We need to get ready, baby."

My father nodded, kissing her cheek. I noticed how his shoulders fell and all his defenses seemed to come down with my mother.

"Essence, let's schedule lunch for this weekend. I expect you to show up," he said as he headed upstairs. "Love you."

"As long as you're alone!" I yelled up the stairs.

My mother sat down at the kitchen counter. We looked at each other and laughed. "Now that he's gone, tell me about this basketball player you're dating."

I stared at her in silence.

"Baby, a mother knows everything. You're glowing, and while your father may not keep up with the devil's world, I can't have my only child working in that industry and not keep up with a blog or two."

I shook my head. "But how'd you know it was me?"

She grabbed her phone out of her bathrobe pocket and opened an article. There was one picture that couldn't be denied. I'm surprised that one got past me.

"I try not to read the blogs because I know 85 percent of it is rumors and speculation," I said. "However, I had been curious about what was out there about us. I didn't see this one."

"Well?"

I tried to relax, hoping I could truly share this moment with my mom. Throughout the years, my mother and I had always been close and there was nothing I couldn't tell her. Even when I had slept with someone when I was seventeen, which was when I lost my virginity, she never told my father. But when I dropped out of seminary to pursue music, they both decided to hold a grudge against me for it. That was when things shifted, and she started taking my father's side when it came to my career choice or love life.

"Listen, baby," my mother started, placing her mug down and grabbing my hands, "I like Clayton, but I've learned that you're going to make your own decisions, and the more we push, you pull away. I'm getting older and I don't want to butt heads with my daughter about decisions she should make for herself. I apologize for any time I haven't been understanding."

I felt the tears sting my eyes as my mother spoke. I hadn't expected any of this, and judging by the look in her eyes, she hadn't expected to say it.

"When I read the blog article, I was upset at first, but I realized you had already taught me years ago that most things on those blogs are lies. But the look of love on your face can't be denied. That's something I want to share with you, not something I have to find out"—she looked down at her phone—"like this."

I nodded. "I honestly just wanted to wait until we were more solid, but you guys haven't made it easy for me to tell you what's going on in my life. Mom, I'm grown. I just turned thirty for God's sake."

"I know, I know," she said, wiping my face. "I promise to do better. And I won't tell your father. I think I'm beginning to see where I went wrong in a lot of areas, b t I'll worry about that. For now, spill the tea. What's he like?"

My mother picked her mug back up and drank her tea and I couldn't help but wonder what God was doing. I mean, here it was, I was still easing into this thing with Shane and my mother was able to see I was happy. As I shared with her how we met and the details of what we had shared so far, I kept some things for myself, but appreciated that we seemed to be getting back to the mama I connected with when I was seventeen.

* * *

"I'M SO SORRY, babe. I know you had a night planned for us, but I have to handle this with my artist."

"Trish can't do it?" he asked, sadness dripping from his voice.

I hated I had to cancel dinner, but Coffee Tan had run into a huge issue with the promoters for the show we booked. Since it was a smaller show, we had handled everything months ago and expected things to go smoothly since it was only a venue that held five thousand. We hired someone to assist him and figured we both could take the night off, but now, the promoter was trying to jam him up and I couldn't let her handle this on her own.

"It's bad, babe. These things happen. Promoters try to change up on the artist when they get to the venue and then try to claim we discussed it. Trish has a family emergency she's been dealing with since last night, so I have to step in."

I heard the heavy sigh on the other end of the phone. I actually wished I could find my way out of this, but I honestly couldn't. Business always came first, no matter how much I was falling in love. There were times I wish business didn't have to come first, but it didn't change that it would.

"I promise I'll make it up to you, and if I can still make it to you in time for dessert, I will."

That was actually the reason I had called him instead of FaceTimed. I didn't want to see the look on his face. He was so excited when he called me this morning with the plans for tonight, and by the sound of the menu, I was already there in my mind.

"It's okay, love," he finally said. "I know the world we're a part of. You were understanding when we had to do a bunch of virtual dates because of my schedule. I got you."

I breathed a sigh of relief. I figured he would understand, but hearing him say it meant a lot. I needed the same grace I'd given him, but it was deeper than that. Now that I'd told my mother about us, I wanted —no—*needed* this to work out.

Eight

SHANE

"SO, Shane, tell me, where do you think the team went wrong this past season? You guys have great scorers, you had the least number of injuries throughout the season compared to other teams, although it did get a little rough toward the end, and there's a unique cohesiveness that you guys play with, yet, you're not going to the playoffs. Enlighten me."

I shifted in my seat as I stared at the ESPN teleprompter. When my coach asked me to represent the team for the post-season interview, I felt it was my duty. Now, as I sat here under the lights that caused sweat beads to drip down my face and back, I wish I had said no.

"Honestly, KJ, I think we just need to strengthen our offense. We've been doing great on defense and our offense has gotten stronger, but I know there's some work we need to do there." I paused. "I love what you said, though. One of the reasons I love playing for Philly is because we have such great camaraderie when we're out there on that floor. We know when to pass the ball, when to take the shot, and we play our hearts out. I wouldn't have wanted to lose with another team."

KJ nodded. "That's the thing I love about the Panthers. When you guys are out there on that floor, there's a team effort that can't be denied. Despite missing some great rebound shots this season, is there anything you think you could've done better to help your team go all the way?"

I licked my lips. I felt my mouth getting drier by the second. "I'm definitely going to be working on my jump shot more and my three-point shot while we're on break, but overall, I think the more I practice during the off season, the better I'll be."

"Well, you're one of my favorite players and MVPs of the last three years," he said, turning to face the camera. "Speaking of MVP, Mickey Rowen is killing it out there, off the court, of course. Ever since he retired, he's opened up more cleaners and car washes than anybody I know. Everyone thought Mickey was crazy for retiring at thirty-two, but he came in, did his ten years, and is now one of the most successful former athletes we know. Watch out, Magic, this kid is on your heels."

"Shane, before we go," KJ continued, turning back to face me, "what are your plans outside of basketball? You're pretty mum when it comes to your private life, but have you been working on anything else? We know you just opened up Mocha Tea & Trends, a tea and coffee shop in Old City, which, by the way, folks, has the best seafood grilled cheese sandwich I've ever tasted. Anything else on your radar?"

I adjusted my tie and took a deep breath. My lips were dry. I cleared my throat. "Well, like you said, I'm pretty mum on my private affairs, so you'll just have to wait. You guys weren't even supposed to know I owned MTT, but what can I say?"

I laughed nervously, hoping the answer would suffice. He caught me completely off guard with that last question, and if I'm honest, I would've rather answered more questions about losing the season.

"Well, that's all for now for my segment. Stay tuned for more sports news and interviews with my colleague, Jeff Winston. I'll see you same time, same place, tomorrow afternoon."

When the producer yelled, "Cut!" I almost flew out of my chair. KJ had been following my career since college and he was definitely great when it came to his job, but him asking me about life outside of basketball had me rattled. I rushed to the bathroom. I looked at myself in the mirror, then splashed water on my face. Leaning against the wall, I realized the anxiety that settled over me whenever I had to think about life outside of basketball was beginning to weigh on me.

It was one thing to fear things changing or to wonder how life would end up, but I was beginning to panic quite a bit whenever I had to consider it. I needed to talk to my therapist before I exploded. After I calmed myself down, I went back out to where KJ was waiting for me.

"There he is," he said, giving me a pound. "Great job today."

I nodded. "Thanks, man. I appreciate you for having me on."

A few of the producers and staff members were getting the set ready for the next segment, so we stepped off to the side.

"Listen, I would love for you to have dinner with my wife and I while you're on break. That's if you can squeeze us in."

I smiled, happy to be discussing something different. "I would love that. Can I bring someone?"

He leaned in, lowering his voice. "It wouldn't happen to be that beautiful woman we've been seeing you with on all the blogs, is it?"

"Actually, it is."

"Is it serious?"

"Let's just say she's been to my place and I'm considering settling down."

I was choosing my words carefully. I knew I could trust KJ, especially because he'd shown me his consistency over the last decade, but I still wanted to protect what we had.

"We aren't ready to go public yet, but I'm happy," I continued.

"That's why I didn't ask you questions about it. Granted, ESPN isn't that type of show, but personal questions do come up."

"I appreciate that, man," I said, checking my phone. "Speaking of, I have to go."

He grinned. "Hey, say less. We'll talk soon."

I headed to the green room to change my clothes. Essence and I were meeting up at Mocha Tea & Trends, then ordering take out for dinner at my place. As I got dressed, I noticed how my heartbeat started returning to its normal pace as I thought about her. If this woman could make my anxiety attacks dissipate like that, she was definitely worth going public for.

* * *

"I THOUGHT the interview went well, babe," Essence said, sipping on her orange blossom tea. "I think you're being too hard on yourself."

I sat back against the chair. We were set up way in the back, away from the crowd, but still in the mix enough not to feel secluded.

"I just hate that I never have an answer for that question."

She placed her tea down. "Never?"

I shrugged. "I mean, it's not like I get asked that all the time, but when I do, I can honestly say I stumble every time."

She reached for my hand, stroking the back of it as she drank some more of her tea. "Let me ask you this. What were your plans with Mocha Tea & Trends?"

"I had a buddy who lives in South Korea who kept telling me about these coffee beans he was growing and how popular they were in Asia. He shipped me some, and once I tasted the coffee, I knew he was on to something. I always wanted to host events and stuff, sort of like an open mic night vibe, so I decided to start with a coffee shop, but I love tea more. It was a great way to combine the two. Restaurants are too competitive, so this made sense."

"And because you had an exclusive coffee distributor, you bought in."

"Exactly."

I was currently drinking one of our most popular coffees, caramel and chocolate bean. I had to admit, my coffee connection had scored big with these beans. If we only served coffee, we would still turn a nice profit, especially since we sold it in bags as well.

"I'm proud of you for taking that leap of faith," Essence continued. "To be honest, coffee is just as competitive, so the fact that you're doing well speaks volumes."

"Baylock wanted me to tell everyone from jump that I owned it. He figured people would flock to it because of my name and that would help sales, but the coffee speaks for itself. The way people found out I owned it was an accident, but I can say it has worked to our advantage."

She smiled.

"What?"

"You're an entrepreneur. You create an atmosphere once a month where celebrities get to have an exclusive experience at a great rate. Most people would have to fly to LA or New York to get something like that. This place is a gem, babe. Trust me, you don't have to have a bunch of different things going on in order for you to see success."

I let what she said sink in. I wasn't trying to be the next Mickey Rowen or Magic Johnson. I knew multiple streams of income were important, especially for an athlete, but to her point, I was on to something already. I knew I would still play for at least another four years and I had time to figure it out.

"I think it's natural for me to be hard on myself, but I appreciate you for encouraging me to see it from another angle," I said, winking at her.

"That's what I'm here for."

As we sat in silence, staring at each other and flirting like teenagers, I took in what I had built. Looking around and seeing the customers happy, working on their laptops and enjoying whatever they purchased made me savor the moment. There were a lot of coffee shops in Philly, especially in Old City, but mine was filled to capacity. I'd been here enough times when people couldn't even find a seat and got frustrated as they left with their freshly brewed coffee. It was a good problem to have.

"I might consider opening up other locations," I blurted, breaking the silence.

"Or franchise it," she responded.

Boom! Boom!

Before I could respond, the double sound that came from outside made me stand up and go to the front door. I looked around, then noticed a large truck trying to make a delivery to a nearby restaurant. Looking up and down the street again, I went back inside. When I sat down, Essence had her hand over her chest and her caramel complexion was a little ashen.

"Baby Girl, you okay?" I asked, grabbing her other hand.

She jumped. "What was that?"

I had to strain just to hear her. "There's a truck making a delivery nearby. They must've dropped something."

I noticed her shaking hand in mine. I squinted, trying to make sense of her reaction.

"Are you sure you're okay?"

She wouldn't take her eyes off me. "Are you sure that's all it was?"

I leaned forward, stroking her face. "Hey, hey. Listen, everything's okay. I promise it was just the truck."

She nodded slowly, then looked down. Picking her tea back up, she drank some more of it. I continued to stroke the hand I held. She placed her cup down but didn't say anything.

"How's the blog coming along?"

She blinked a few times, but I had to repeat my question before she answered.

"It's good. I haven't published the first post yet, but I have written a few. I'll publish the first one soon."

"Can I read one of them?"

"Uh, actually, yeah. That's not a bad idea," she said, her shoulders finally relaxing.

She looked outside the window behind me, then looked back down at her tea. I wanted to pry, but something about her reaction told me this wasn't just about growing up in Philly, traumatized by the gun violence. It was deeper than that. Part of being patient was giving her the space to share what she wanted, when she wanted. While it wasn't easy, it was necessary.

* * *

"HOW WAS YOUR FOOD, BABY?" I asked Essence as I washed off our plates.

We had just finished our takeout, which was delicious. Danny Wok's fried chicken with shrimp lo mein was perfect. While I cheated here and there during the season, being able to cheat just a little more during the off season was everything. I wasn't a huge junk food guy, just a lover of soul food, fried anything and home-cooked meals.

She sat at the kitchen counter, still zoned out from earlier. I tried making small talk, but she had me worried now. There was never a moment where she hadn't been able to keep a conversation going or even if we had a small disagreement, bounce back and find her groove.

Whatever happened at Mocha Tea & Trends regarding that sound had really bothered her.

"Baby," I called out. She looked at me.

She laughed nervously. "I'm sorry, babe. What did you say?"

"How was your food?"

"It was good. Danny Wok's never disappoints."

I turned the water off. Drying my hands on the dish towel, I walked over to her and grabbed her in a hug from behind.

"You know I'll wait until you're ready, but what happened back there?"

I felt her body stiffen up.

"Nothing. It just caught me off guard."

I walked around and sat across from her at the counter. "Baby, we grew up hearing gunshots and loud noises. That's the hood life. The way you reacted was different."

She closed her eyes, taking a deep breath, then opened them. "Something happened in my childhood that I'm not ready to discuss yet. I promise when the time is right, I'll tell you."

I nodded. That made me feel a little better. I could only imagine what it was, but at least I knew where it started. Discussing old childhood wounds were never easy. I grabbed her hand, kissed it, then led her into the dining room.

"It's raining. How about I turn on the fireplace and we sit here and talk? Nothing deep, we can just shoot the breeze."

She looked up at me. "I'd like that."

I grabbed a few pieces of cut up wood that was by the fireplace and started the fire. I kept chopped up wood during the cooler months. It was late spring, but with the rainy nights, lighting a fire was perfect for this type of weather. Once I sat back down, she got comfortable, lying in my arms with the blanket thrown over her legs.

"Can I ask you something?" she asked.

"Anything."

"How do you open up so easily? You're very vulnerable in ways I wish I could be. Where did you get that from?"

I thought about it for a second. "When I was younger, my father and I would talk all the time about everything. There wasn't any subject off limits. Even my mother and I would talk about stuff that most boys wouldn't talk about with their mothers. You know how some households had that rule that what goes on in this house stays in this house?"

"Yeah. Unfortunately."

"Well, that wasn't us. My parents were big on communication. If something hurt you, you tell someone. Even if it was them that caused the pain. It's crazy how that stayed with me. I remember having assignments throughout grade school and well into college where I would have to talk on a subject or write some kind of paper. I never shied away from those moments."

She shifted her position so she was now looking at me. "I envy you."

I chuckled. "You don't have to envy me, baby. You can be vulnerable."

She gagged, putting her finger in her mouth as if she was throwing up. This made me laugh harder. I was happy to see her returning to her normal, playful self.

"You know what I mean. Listen," I said, wrapping her back in my arms. "I don't open up to everyone. There are players on my team that only know my name and stats, and it'll stay that way because I don't feel comfortable opening up to them. Then, there's Kevell and Reggie, who I trust with my life. They may be a little immature when it comes to women, and they get drunk from time to time, but I trust them."

The rain pattered against the windows, coming down harder than it was before. I listened to the rhythm of the rain for a minute before continuing.

"The world is cold. Everybody wants to be hard and hide their feelings. I don't have the capacity to be fake. I want to be me, and if that means some people think I wear my heart on my sleeves, then I'm okay with that. Being vulnerable and transparent has allowed me to walk in a freedom I can't explain."

"That's really powerful, babe. I guess my household was different. I have people I trust, but sometimes, opening up for me is hard. I think about what the person will do with the information I'm giving them."

I frowned when she said that. It was hard not taking stuff like that personally, but I realized there were still pieces of her past I had yet to explore or be privy to. I couldn't take everything to heart.

"We both trust God and we know how to use our discernment. I want you to feel comfortable with me. Only you can tell when it's time to let me into all the parts of your heart."

She was silent, but I could tell she was still with me. She ran her finger gently up and down my arm. We chatted for another hour, and when I heard the light snores coming from the tender body lying in my arms, I kissed her forehead, then pulled the blanket up closer to her chin. For now, I was content with the fact she trusted me enough to let me hold her like this and to be there for her. It was a start.

Nine

ESSENCE

"GIRL, and did you see how she responded to that email? I'm starting to regret signing her," Trish said, handing me some more napkins.

We were having lunch in our office, discussing business, as usual. Sadly, we were starting to notice Remi's diva ways. She'd only been with us a few weeks and we were starting to regret signing her.

"Do you think she's just pushing the envelope? Seeing how far she can go with us?"

"I don't have time for games," Trish responded. "I hope that's not what she's doing. I'm all for an artist making sure they give their label and management a trial run, just like we do them, but be mature about it."

"Yeah. You know how direct I am, so I expect the same from others."

Remi had already been booked for two major gigs since being with us and her demands for the venues were off the charts. This girl acted like she was Beyoncé performing at Coachella. She was a great artist who had a substantial following, but she had a long way to go before she could demand all yellow M&Ms in her dressing room or a marching band to welcome her into the venue. While she hadn't asked for those things per se, her demands were dramatic.

"Did you see her face when the promoter said no to her request for three assistants? One to help her get ready, one to help her with the outfits when she went to the bathroom, and another to fan her so she wouldn't sweat off her makeup?"

I laughed as I took another bite of my sandwich. "Mariah would never," I teased.

"Well, all we can do is let her ride these ninety days out. I just hope things don't get worse."

I shook my head. "Let's just hope our email and our FaceTime conversation made her realize we aren't to be played with. You have Grammys and you don't even act like that."

We continued discussing other business matters over dinner, then switched to our personal lives.

"So, how are things going with Shane? Girl, you snagged a good one. I saw his feature in GQ for last month. He is fine."

"Why thank you, ma'am," I said, clearly blushing. "Things are good. Better than I expected. We're flowing."

She took another bite of her sushi. "Things with Maurice and I are going well. Really well. I mean, we've had a few disagreements, but I honestly can't find anything wrong. Well... there is one thing."

"Uh oh. What?"

"He's not open to going to therapy."

I let out a heavy breath. "Oh. Girl, we can work with that. I thought you were going to tell me he liked men or something."

She threw a balled-up napkin at me. "As if I would be this calm."

"Did he say why?"

"I think it has something to do with his childhood, which I'm really protective about. He's shared some things with me that are pretty heavy, but I know he needs to talk to someone."

I nodded, sipping my iced tea. "Maybe God placed you in his life to help him get there. As long as it's not a project where you're rebuilding this man, I say stick it out. Therapy isn't the first thing we run to as Black people, so I can understand his resistance."

"But you know how I am about mental health. I literally talk about it all the time. It sucks to be dating someone that is so opposed to it."

I leaned back in my chair. "So, does he criticize others who go or say negative things, or does he just feel it's not for him?"

"He isn't negative about others who are in therapy, and he isn't really critical, but I feel like I have to tread lightly when talking about it."

"I see. Well, as long as he's supportive of you going and he isn't being critical, I believe this might be what Shane and I were talking about the other night."

She finished the last of her sushi, then threw the plate in the bag we would throw out later. "What were you guys talking about?"

"You remember what I shared with you about my childhood when we first got close?"

She nodded.

"I still haven't told him, but I was triggered the other day. Bad. Anyway, we were back at his place and it made me ask him how he opens up so easily. When I tell you, I have a Dr. Phil mixed with Tupac on my hands, I'm not lying. He's like a spiritual thug."

Trish started laughing, causing me to laugh.

"I mean, that's the best way to explain it. So, he mentioned how he loves being vulnerable and transparent because the world has enough cold people. Then he said something that left me stuck."

"Spill," she said, leaning closer to me.

"He said he realized that one of the problems in his last relationship was that she was looking for a finished product, but he was willing to take her how she was and help her with the areas she struggled in. Do we as women really expect for these men to come to us with no issues, but expect them to help us with ours?"

We sat in silence for a few minutes. It was a deep question. When Shane had said it the other night, he was just telling me a story, so I listened, but it made me think about it once I got home.

"Well, do you?" Trish asked, disrupting my thoughts.

"Honestly, no. I take Shane as he is. His vulnerability actually rubs up against me quite a bit, because that's not who I am, but I appreciate that it's who he is. I also know there are other challenges he has, but I guess if there's one thing Bishop Taylor taught me, it's how to take a man in the many forms he comes in."

She nodded, but didn't say anything. We finished our lunch in silence, checking our phones as we prepared to jump back into work mode. Shane was teaching me a lot and not just about vulnerability. He had a good head on his shoulders, and I knew he could have any woman he wanted, women who would probably tell him their life story from A to Z, just because he was such a good listener. Yet, he wanted me, and he was giving me the patience I always wished my father had given me. I picked up my phone and texted him. I wanted to show him just how much I appreciated him.

* * *

"WOW, BABY. THIS LOOKS GREAT," Shane said, walking around to kiss my neck. "When you texted me to come by for a little surprise, I wasn't expecting a full-course meal."

I turned around and kissed him gently. "Anything for you, babe."

I moved the pots and pans around, finalizing dinner. I kept it simple, but the aromas alone had me ready to dig in. I made seafood alfredo with scallops and crawfish, since most people only made it with two or three seafood options. I also made homemade garlic bread, a garden salad and pound cake for dessert. The conversation I had with Trish made me think about how there were certainly times we could be hard on our men.

After our conversation, we prayed together and made a promise to not run from the love we were experiencing. Now, as I stood here watching him try to sneak a shrimp from the leftover shrimp I had made, I couldn't help but thank God for that talk.

"Stop digging," I scolded. "I only cooked them because I had them thawed already. I may make something for me tomorrow."

He backed away. "Sorry, gorgeous. I can't help it if I love your cooking."

He helped me finish setting everything on the table, then pulled out my chair so I could sit down. "You've done enough. Relax."

"Okay, okay," I said, rolling up the sleeves on my sweater. "Can you bless the food?"

He prayed, then started dipping food on my plate before helping himself. An hour into dinner, we were laughing and going over our last few months as a couple.

"So, are you saying you're ready to go public?"

I sighed. "Maybe at the next red-carpet event? We're attending the Black Women in Music Awards together, right?"

"In July? Yeah. I would love to be your plus one," he said. "I honestly forgot about it. I'm glad you reminded me."

"I'll send you the information. Please lock it in, babe."

"I promise I won't forget."

"But to answer your question, since the blogs are talking about us, we need to tell our own story."

"Sounds good. We can pray about it just to make sure we have peace about it. The blogs don't get to dictate our timing."

I had to appreciate how protective he was. He'd been this way since day one. There was a difference between a man who hid you and a man who protected you. Shane was making sure the media wouldn't have a field day with my heart and I was grateful for it. We finished dinner, with him getting seconds and me holding out for the pound cake I made.

"Babe, can you change that song while I cut our dessert? Something more upbeat," I hollered out to him from the kitchen. "You want ice cream with yours?"

"Is there any other way to eat pound cake?" he shouted back.

We'd been chilling out to a cool jazz playlist on Spotify, but I wanted to jam a little bit. I heard silence, then nothing. I frowned, not sure why it would take him that long to change the station. I placed the pound cake on the counter, then peeked around the kitchen wall into the living room.

"You good? R&B is fine."

I looked at his face, then slowly walked over to him.

"Clayton wants to know when you guys can do dinner."

My heart dropped in my stomach. I had been ignoring Clayton, literally not responding to any of his messages, but I also hadn't blocked him.

"Babe, it's not like that."

He placed my phone down. "What is it like, Essence?"

THE ESSENCE OF HIS SOUL

I raised an eyebrow. Since we'd been dating, he barely called me by my first name.

I walked over to him, grabbing his hands. He let me. "My father thinks Clayton is the guy I should be dating. I told him I was dating but haven't told him who, but my mother knows. Clayton and I went on a date four years ago and I haven't talked to him since. My father thought giving him my number when he ran into him was a good idea."

He stared at me intently. This was the first time he was looking at me and I didn't feel the warmth I usually felt. "Baby, I promise, you have nothing to worry about."

"You know Rayna DM'd me about a week after we started dating. I blocked her because, even though we weren't that deep yet, I knew we were on to something."

I swallowed. I knew he was all in when we were on our third date. Shane was definitely a one-woman type of man. I picked up my phone and blocked Clayton in front of him. Then I showed him the text thread.

"You can see I never even responded."

"Then why not block him sooner?" he said, scrolling through the texts.

I started chewing on my bottom lip. I brushed my hair behind my ears, trying not to speak too soon.

"If I'm honest, this is scary for me. I'm afraid that this thing with you and I won't work out. That's not to say Clayton was a backup, because he knows that even if he was the last man standing, there would never be an us. Trust me."

He smirked, placing the phone back on the counter. "He's that bad?"

"Horrible."

I laughed. He was still staring at me, but his smile faded.

"I don't always feel safe," I continued, hoping the rest of this would come out making sense, "and some of it has to do with what happened when I was younger. I also feel like my father's controlling ways plays into how unsafe I feel. It's like he would never let anyone else hurt me, yet he does it all the time; and then, there's what my ex did."

His face scrunched up. "Dixon?"

I'd told him bits and pieces, but not the deep stuff. "My father got a woman pregnant way before my parents had their church. She ended up having an abortion and my father kind of made it go away. I shared it with Dixon when we were six months into dating, thinking I could trust him. Two weeks later, I had three blogs emailing me about my father's secret life."

His face softened. "Wow. Why would he do that?"

"I think he could tell I would never be the chick that was completely dependent on a man. He wasn't as bad as Clayton when it comes to expecting a woman to sit at home and cater to all of her man's needs, but he was still very traditional. The more he pushed, the more I pulled away and continued to focus on my career. I think he told someone in confidence, but he was venting about me. I guess he couldn't trust them either."

He nodded. "I still don't know if that explains why you didn't block Clayton, but I'm trying to not get upset since you didn't respond to him."

"Can I be honest and just say I wasn't thinking about him? Every message that came through, I just flagged it off. There was no specific reason why I hadn't blocked him."

I felt the tears welling up in my eyes. If there was one thing I had learned about Shane, it was that he expected honesty and loyalty, mainly because that was what he gave you. He'd been hurt enough, and I hadn't meant to add to his pain.

I grabbed the back of his head and rested his forehead on mine. "I apologize. I would never do anything to hurt you. I would leave you before I hurt you," I said softly. "I just wasn't thinking. Maybe I got some kick out of ignoring him because I know my father wants us together and a part of me loves rebelling against my dad. But no matter what, I have no desire to be with anyone else."

I picked my phone up and handed it to him. "You can have my passcode and check. I promise—"

"Don't do that," he said, shoving the phone back at me. "I trust you. I believe you." He grabbed me close to him. "Essence, you have to talk to your dad. This isn't healthy. I know he may be overbearing, but at some point, he's going to learn about us. It needs to be through you."

He lifted my chin lightly, so we were looking into each other's eyes. "I can be patient about a lot of things, but once we decide to go public, I'm not hiding our relationship from anyone. So, you may want to have that talk with your dad ASAP."

He grabbed me close, throwing his arms around my waist. "There's not another woman that thinks she has a chance with me because I don't play about you. You better make sure no other man thinks he has a chance with you. Period."

I nodded, kissing him and falling into the moment. The way he spoke was authoritative but loving. He was letting me know that from this moment on, it was just us. For the first time in my life, I was okay with a man telling me what to do.

Ten

SHANE

THROWING THE COVERS BACK, I slowly got up to get my day started. I could already feel the weight of the day on me as I stood up and stretched. I hadn't been to therapy in a few months, namely because I hadn't really needed it, but I was going today. I knew I couldn't keep running from how I felt about life outside of basketball. After we prayed over our relationship last night, Essence covered me in prayer, specifically touching on God helping me realize my identity outside of the game.

I slowly trudged to the bathroom, grabbing my portable speaker and phone to play some music. Turning on Maverick City Music, I allowed the worship song to take over my endless thoughts. *When a multitude of anxious thoughts are within me, your comforts delight my soul.* I meditated on one of my favorite Bible verses, mumbling it over and over under my breath as I turned the shower on.

As I stood under the water, I closed my eyes and thought about this past season. Everything I depended on revolved around basketball: my friendships, business opportunities, which included endorsements, and even any speaking opportunities. They were all tied to my role as a basketball player. This was going to be harder than I imagined, but therapy was a good start. My therapist was a former NFL player turned therapist who definitely would understand what I was going through.

After spending close to an hour in the shower, wasting water and time, I finally shut it off. My appointment wasn't until the afternoon, but I knew if I waited to get ready, I would end up rescheduling out of fear. As I got dressed, I changed the music to a worship instrumental album that I had come to love. I didn't want to hear words right now. I needed to hear from God. My phone buzzed, disrupting the music. I didn't want to be distracted, but I had a feeling it was who I needed right now.

Good morning, babe. I've been praying for you all morning. I'm glad I decided to work from home today because I can't stop thinking about you. How are you feeling? How's your heart?

I felt the heaviness coming back, but I brushed it off. Essence was the one person who I would share everything with.

Honestly, I'm scared of what will come up in therapy. I know it's not, but I feel like the conversation I'll have with him is about an ending I'm not ready for.

Don't look at it that way, babe. It's just a conversation about who you are outside of the game and who you want to be. That doesn't mean when you figure it out, you have to retire, silly.

I chuckled. I knew I was overthinking it, but who could blame me?

I promise to call when it's over. Let me get back to worshipping. I love you.

I love you. Take your time when it's over. You may need to process the conversation before calling me.

I was so worried about my session, I hadn't realized I said 'I love you' for the first time. What was even more surprising was that she said it back without skipping a beat. Maybe today wouldn't be so bad after all.

* * *

"YOU KNOW you're preaching to the choir, right?" Nathan asked, laughing. "I spent three years trying to live in my glory days before God had had enough. At least you're in a place where you're searching for the answers you'll need later. That takes courage."

I forced a smile. "Yeah. I guess so."

He grabbed his notepad and a pen, then looked at me again. "Tell me what you did growing up when you weren't playing basketball."

I got comfortable. "I used to draw, sometimes. I was no Michelangelo, but I was pretty good. I spent a lot of time outside as a kid, doing boy stuff: throwing rocks, playing with snails, stuff like that."

"Anything else come to mind? Anything where you found yourself excited to get back to it?"

"I read a lot."

He jotted something down. I looked at the clock on the wall as he wrote.

"Okay. Let's dig deeper. I think what's more important than finding something else to do when you're not playing basketball, is to figure out who you are. I don't want you to go finding a bunch of activities to do just to kill time. Who you are is the one thing that won't change, no matter what you do."

I nodded. "So, how do we do that?"

"Tell me about Shane. The Shane nobody knows."

I frowned. "I don't get it."

"That's the point. This isn't going to be a one-off session, Shane. You need to know who you are. Of course, as believers, we know our identity is rooted in Christ. That's a given. But if you aren't sure what that identity looks like for you, you'll always let others define you."

He leaned forward, placing the notepad and pen on the table that sat between us. "So, who is Shane Bishop?"

I swallowed the lump that had formed in my throat and took a deep breath. It was now or never.

* * *

I HAD TO BE HONEST. The session wasn't all bad. Once we went through a couple of exercises to help me get to the core of who I am, it flowed pretty well. I looked forward to next week's session. I actu-

THE ESSENCE OF HIS SOUL

ally couldn't wait to get home to work on the homework I had. For now, I was headed to my parents. I'd been spending a lot of time with them since the season ended, but I definitely wanted to tell them about Essence.

They knew I was seeing her, but I wanted them to know I felt like I'd found the one. As angry as I wanted to be with her about the Clayton situation, I knew she was being honest with me. I also knew what I had, and if I was Clayton, I wouldn't give up either. Essence wasn't the type of woman you let get away. That was why it was our job to block people from thinking they had access to us.

I pulled into my parents' townhome in Chestnut Hill, a nice area in Philadelphia. I'd bought them a new home during my first year in the league. They wanted something small and comfortable and that was exactly what they got. That was actually where I got my low-key lifestyle from. My father had done real estate all my life, in addition to being a pastor, and my mother was a nurse anesthetist. My parents had money when we were growing up, but they taught us the value of a dollar.

"Pop!" I yelled as I entered the foyer. "You in here, old man?"

I knew they were home because both of their cars were in the driveway.

My mother came walking out of the kitchen, arms open wide.

"Son," she said, pecking both of my cheeks. "What are you doing here?"

"I can't come see my parents when I want to?"

She grinned. "Of course, you can. If it were up to me, you would still live here."

I looked around, walking into the living room. "Where's Pop?"

I turned around just as she looked upstairs. "He's not feeling too well today, but he'll be down."

I stopped smiling. When I came to visit my parents a couple of months ago, it came out that my father had some heart issues. It made sense why he was acting so distracted whenever Sahana and I were around. He was trying to hide it. I'd been staying on him about his medication, and since the season had ended, I walked with him on Saturday mornings so he could get a good workout in.

"Has he been doing everything he's supposed to?"

She nodded. "And I've been preparing healthier meals. He's eating them, I just think he's tired."

I felt my stomach drop when she said 'tired'. Whenever someone said that, it made me think they were ready to go home to be with the Lord. I wasn't ready for Pop to leave me.

"He'll be fine. He just has to stay healthy and keep serving God like he's been doing," I said, getting ready to head upstairs.

"Hey, Son," my pop said, standing at the top of the stairs. "I was coming. I got your text."

He actually looked pretty good—his complexion had returned, and he was standing straight. Last time, he looked pale and he was slightly bent over. I beamed as he landed on the bottom step. I grabbed my old man in a bear hug, picking him up off the bottom step.

"Put him down," my mother scolded, laughing just as hard as my father.

I placed him down on the floor. "What are we getting into today?"

We all walked over to the couch and sat down. "Well, Son, you said you had some good news in your text. What's going on?"

I smiled. "Essence."

"The young lady you've been seeing?" my mother asked.

I nodded. "Dad, I really believe she's the one. We've had a unique flow to our courtship since day one, and even when we have challenges, we literally work through them peacefully. It's a blessing and kind of strange all at the same time."

He looked at my mother, then back at me. "Sounds like you're in love. I felt that way about your mother."

He launched into the story about how he knew my mother was the one and how he never wanted to be with anyone after they had met. They broke up once in college, but they ended up right back together when they realized there was nobody else out there for them. We laughed and talked for the next few hours, with me sharing photos from my phone of Essence and I, along with a few from our top dates. I even stayed for dinner, which was the perfect way to end my day.

Of course, there was one more thing I needed to end my day: to talk to the love of my life. I texted her after the session, but she wanted me to enjoy my day with my parents. As I pulled out of my parents' driveway, it started raining. At first, it was a steady rain, but within ten minutes, it was pouring. I turned my wipers on a higher speed, then called Essence.

"Hey, my love," I said as soon as she answered.

I felt good. The day had started out a little heavy but ended up being one of the best days I'd had since the season ended.

"Hey, baby. You sound light. You must've had some good cooking at your parents'."

"It was everything I needed. Today was good, hon. Even with all my fears and concerns, it actually ended up going really well."

I heard her clapping in the background. "I'm happy for you. I was praying for you throughout the day. I didn't want you worrying."

"Nothing like a praying woman," I said, trying to see through the rain. "Listen, babe, it's raining pretty heavy out here. I'll call you as soon as I get in."

"It just stopped raining over here. Crazy how it can be raining cats and dogs in one area of Philly, but not raining in another. Be safe."

"Tell me about it. Talk to you soon, sweets."

I ended the call. I hadn't even placed my phone on the charger yet. I stopped at a light, then grabbed the charger to plug my phone up. My notifications went off. I thought I still had my phone on silent. Since I was stopped, I opened the Instagram app to see what it was. I had a message.

It can wait, I thought. As soon as the light turned green, I made my way through the traffic to drive the twenty-five minutes to my place. When I pulled into my garage, the rain had slacked up quite a bit. Grabbing my phone, I decided to check the message before I got inside. When I saw it had come from a woman, I started to delete it without reading it, but the first line caught my attention.

Hi, Shane. I hate jumping in your inbox like this, but I haven't been able to reach you through your parents. I know this is super weird and you're probably used to getting all kinds of crazy messages in your inbox, but I've been trying to find you for some time now. My name is Casey. Casey Kirkwood. I'm your younger sister. I would prefer to discuss off-line. Here's my number. Please. Let me explain.

I read the message at least three times before I closed my garage door and got out. Just as I placed my hand on the knob that led to my kitchen, I heard thundering and more rain. It was raining heavy again. I guess it was true what they say; when it rains, it pours.

Eleven

ESSENCE

I'VE NEVER BEEN *this happy in a relationship before. I know we seem to say that all the time when we meet somebody new, but the truth is, you know what real happiness feels like when you stumble upon it. I say stumble, because I wasn't looking for love when I met Shane. I guess you can say I was ready for it, though. And that's the place I want you all to be. Ready for the love God wants to send, not looking for it or running from it because the last one hurt you. Be open to what God wants to do through your love story. I'm waiting for the rest to unfold, but here are a few tips to help you heal from that last heartbreak and step into the new God has for you.*

I SAVED what I had written so far and closed my laptop. It was my day off and I decided to have lunch with my father. I would publish the post after I completed it and after we had our talk. He was going to learn about my relationship today and I was actually looking forward to the conversation. I know from the outside looking in, it appeared I was afraid of my father, but I just didn't have the energy to explain myself. It was better to just live my life and let him find out when he did. I let him be upset for as long as he needed to, then, he eventually got over it.

But I didn't want to keep living like that. I figured the best way to change this was to go back to the way things were before I dropped out of seminary—having a daddy-daughter outing. My mother checked in regularly ever since I had told her, and she genuinely showed support. I knew it wouldn't take much for her to get on board. My father, on the other hand, would take the prayers of all the church mothers in America, along with a miracle.

I grabbed my bag and phone, then headed out to my car. I was still tired from staying up until three in the morning, talking to Shane. We actually discussed the 'I love you' moment we had. I was honest with him about how easy it was to love him. It was easy for me to say it back because I meant it, and I knew he did. For the last several months, he'd shown me love. Even the rebirth of my blog was evidence of that. I was opening up about my relationship to my paid subscribers, which was about five hundred women.

Which was why I wasn't going to publish this last post until after I talked to my father. I smiled as I pulled into traffic, grateful for the beautiful, sunny day. I'd chosen Benny's Soul Food for my father and me to have lunch at. They had just started opening during lunch hours a year ago, which was perfect since it was one of his favorite spots. He was a health nut, but when he did eat soul food, this was where he preferred to go. I guess you could say I was trying to butter him up.

It really didn't matter how he responded. He would have to deal with that on his own. I was a bit nervous last night, but after Shane prayed with me and then I prayed again when we hung up, I felt better. I wasn't going to lie, the little girl in me wanted my father's acceptance. I'd always longed to hear him say he was proud of me, but since pursuing a career in music, I hadn't heard those words from him. It felt like I just kept letting my dad down, but one of my pet peeves was seeing women building their lives to make men happy. As much as I wanted to be a daddy's girl again, I didn't want it at the expense of my happiness.

* * *

"OPENING FOR LUNCH was the best thing you guys could've ever done," my father said, handing the waitress the menu.

I hoped he'd keep this upbeat attitude up.

"Thank you," I said, as she walked away.

"So, your mother is doing better these days," he started, placing his phone face down on the table.

I raised an eyebrow. Pleasantly surprised, I looked at him. "Yes, she told me her blood work came back clear again and everything is looking up. Praise God for that."

He nodded. "Baby Girl, you know your mother is the glue that holds my life together. I don't want to even think about what would happen if..."

I blinked a few times. He was completely catching me off guard, but hearing the way he talked about my mother made me melt inside. This was the daddy I missed, the one who wasn't afraid to share his emotions. I reached for his hand, giving it a reassuring squeeze.

"God ain't done with either of you, so don't even worry."

He winked at me. "What's going on with you? You made some time for your old man, I see."

A few people at a nearby table waved at us. My father smiled and waved back. I was used to this. With a ministry over twenty years old, my parents rarely went anywhere without someone knowing who they were. He turned his attention back to me.

"Clayton says you blocked him."

I didn't know what made me think this would be a normal conversation. I shook my head, but stayed focused.

"Dad, I'm in a loving relationship with someone. I told you before, Clayton wasn't an option."

"So, the rumors are true?"

I let out a heavy sigh. "Yes. I'm with Shane Bishop."

He sat back in his chair. He looked around, then leaned forward. "What do you see in him? He's a basketball player for Christ's sake."

"He's a man of God, who prays with me more than Clayton ever did—"

"You never even gave him a chance. You talked to him, what, three times on the phone and went on one date," he huffed.

"Well, wasn't it you that said you know them by their fruit? It doesn't take three phone calls to initiate prayer."

He glared at me. "Don't be smart."

"Dad, I wanted us to try to have a nice daddy-daughter lunch date so I could tell you what's going on in my life. You're the one making it difficult."

The waitress came back to the table, placing the cornbread down in the center, along with our drinks and some napkins. "Let me know if you need anything else."

I thanked her, then continued.

"You know what I think this is all about?"

He cut two slices of the cornbread, placing one on a plate for me and the other for him. "What what is about?"

I watched him bite into the cornbread. "I dropped out of seminary and you didn't talk to me for three months. Are you that upset that I didn't want to follow in your footsteps?"

He sipped his water. "I could deal with that. You were studying business and had taken a few law classes. I thought you were at least going to pursue a career that was more promising."

I sucked my teeth. "You mean more holy, right?"

He crossed his arms across his chest. I could tell he was seething by the way his chest moved up and down. Silence fell in between us for a few minutes, then I continued.

"Once you realized I wasn't going to follow in your footsteps, you honestly didn't care what career I chose, as long as it didn't tarnish the Taylor name."

"Essence—"

"No, let's be honest, Dad. Isn't that what this is about? The fact that I named my business after our family name and you want nothing to do with the devil's den."

He slammed his hand down on the table. "Enough."

I looked around the restaurant at the few people who were now staring at us. As upset as I was getting, I didn't want my father to have an embarrassing moment he would have to explain later. I picked up my cornbread and ate it, chewing off small pieces until it was gone. The waitress returned with our food ten minutes later. After my father blessed the food, we ate in silence. I was trying to enjoy my meal, but every time I took a bite, I kept thinking about how left our conversation had gone and I literally got sick to my stomach.

"I'll just take mine to go," I said softly.

He had pretty much cleared his plate. I thought about all the times my mother and I had eaten dinner alone, with her barely able to finish her food, while he walked in, expecting his plate to be made hours later. This was just like him. He caused frustration and pain, only to be able to move on and enjoy his life as if nothing happened.

"Out of all your options," he finally spoke, "you're going to choose a basketball player who probably has God knows how many groupies, possibly girlfriends, and probably doesn't even have a plan for when he's done playing ball?"

That last part made me look at him. How did he even know that?

"Dad, I thought you liked Pastor Bishop? Shane comes from a great family and you've spoken at the church his father is a pastor at before."

"Lawrence Bishop and Lady Bishop are fine people. Some of the best. That doesn't mean their son is worthy of my daughter's attention."

I chuckled. "Don't you dare make this about me. You know you're more concerned about how this makes you look than how it affects me."

"That's not true. What does he offer you? You still haven't told me that."

"I know it won't matter, but to answer your question, something that you haven't been able to offer me for years: safety and peace. Ever since I strayed away from your little plan, you haven't made me feel safe enough to come to you for anything other than connections. When was the last time you called to actually pray with me, Daddy, huh? When?"

He didn't budge.

"Exactly. This basketball player that you don't want me with has prayed with me more times than my father has in the last few months. In fact, he's prayed with me more than you have in the last several years." I waved the waitress over. "Can I have a to-go box and the check, please?"

My father still hadn't moved when she came back over with the box and check. I was trying to be gentle with how I came at him and, to be honest, none of this other stuff was supposed to come up, but he opened the door.

"All I'm saying is, don't judge a book by its cover, and definitely not when you haven't been such a great influence yourself. You pray more with your church family than you do your own daughter."

"You barely make time for me," he finally said.

It was my turn to slam my hand down. "This is the first time you've ever turned your phone face down when you've been with us. I almost fainted when you did it. So, don't talk to me about time."

I placed my credit card in the black book, then grabbed my bag. I wasn't going to storm out, but I was trying to stay respectful and it was becoming harder by the second.

"I don't know what's gotten into you, but you've never talked to me like this."

I shook my head. "After everything I just said, that's all you came up with?"

We stared at each other for what felt like hours. I could tell by the look in his eyes that my father wasn't going to give me his blessing, but there was one thing I was leaving the restaurant with: My dignity. He knew I had spoken nothing but facts, and he would have to deal with that. I just prayed for his sake that he came to terms with the truth before God gave him a reality check.

* * *

BACK IN THE CAR, I tried to keep it together. I hadn't meant to cry, especially since I rarely did, but my father was so stubborn, it was maddening. I didn't want to bother him since I knew we were going to meet up later, but I needed to see him now.

"Hi, babe. Where are you?" I said, when he answered. I did my best not to let him hear the tears in my voice.

"What's wrong? Are you okay?"

"It's... just my dad. Listen, I know we were supposed to meet later, but can we meet now? I really need you."

Vulnerability had set in, but I wasn't going to fight it.

"Of course. I actually wanted to talk to you about something, so just come to my place. We can just hang out for the rest of the day."

I wiped at my face. "What's wrong?"

"I should've told you last night, but I wasn't sure what to think of it. It's probably nothing, but since it happened, I might as well tell someone."

"What, babe?"

"I got a DM last night from a woman claiming to be my sister. She said she actually tried reaching me through my parents but hadn't been able to."

I tried to stifle my laugh. "That's crazy. I mean, if she was your sister, that would mean your parents would have to know about her. Probably a money thing."

"That's what I was thinking, but I've been lurking on her page. Let's just say, it's interesting."

I started my car. "Okay, I'm on my way. Between my father and his wicked ways and this girl claiming to be your sister, the enemy is certainly throwing everything he can at us right now."

"Yeah, but you said it right. At us. We're in this together."

After we ended the call, I made my way to his place. I wasn't sure what was going on, but I knew one thing for sure; I'd watched my parents stand and win a couple of battles the enemy had thrown at them. I had five smooth stones ready to go.

Twelve

SHANE

I WALKED INTO DAVE & Buster's and looked around for my sister. I was happy she'd chosen to meet up here. When we were younger, Dave & Buster's was our go-to spot whenever we were frustrated with our parents or when we just needed to get away. Once I spotted her, I headed over to where she sat at the bar, waving at people as I passed by. It would never get old that everywhere I went, people recognized me.

"Well, you're actually on time today," she teased, standing up to hug me.

I wrapped her in a big bear hug, happy to catch up. I definitely wanted to talk to her about the DM. Essence and I had prayed about it, and for now, I decided to leave it alone until I had more information. People would do anything for money and attention these days. Still, there was something about the message that left me tossing and turning at night, unable to rest.

"You look cute," I said.

"Thanks, bro. I've been trying new looks. I actually hired a stylist to help me."

I frowned. "For what? Your look was fine before."

She shrugged. "Just having fun. Honestly, being a lawyer means I have to represent myself and the firm I work for well. I was always a tomboy. Needed a more refined look."

I nodded, then grabbed a menu. After we ordered our food, we continued making small talk, then I switched gears.

"I got a DM the other day," I started, pulling out my phone. I handed it to her.

I watched her eyes bulge as she read the message.

"Money?"

"Not sure. What do you think?"

She looked at my phone again. "It's clear she's lying." She eyed me carefully. "Don't tell me you actually bought into this?"

I stared at my sister, wanting to say I knew for sure the girl was lying, but my spirit wasn't at peace with that answer.

"This just feels weird. I've been in the league six years and all of a sudden, someone pops up. Why now?"

She leaned closer to me. "I don't know, but our parents have been together for decades. There's no way. They would've told us if they'd given up a child for adoption or something."

I grabbed my glass of water. Before taking a sip, I responded. "Would they?"

Sahana's mouth fell open. "Shane... what are you saying?"

I took a few gulps, then placed my glass back down. "Why would she give me a number to call, knowing I could afford to have people look into her? You're a lawyer. Shoot, I could have you look into her. She knows I'll do my homework."

She crossed her arms and squinted. "So, you think there has to be something to this if she's willing to get on the phone?"

"I think it's worth figuring out what's going on. Trust me. I ignored it at first, but her words... they feel, I don't know... real."

Sahana nodded. "What did Essence say?"

I smiled. "How do you know I told her?"

"Because you just smiled like a Cheshire cat. I've seen you glowing."

"Men don't glow." I smiled again. "But, to your point, I'm very happy and I think this is it for me."

She shoved me playfully. "What? Look at you."

A few kids ran past us with their parents fast on their heels. It was a little after two on a Saturday, so the place was definitely going to get crowded soon.

"I love her faith. Her blog is really powerful," she continued.

"You read her blog?"

She nodded. "Yeah. I didn't realize it was such a big deal, but of course, I'm following her on social because she's in my big brother's life. When she announced the return, I subscribed. I even read some of her older posts. She has a way with words."

I stared straight ahead. As Sahana spoke, I beamed with pride. "She does. Just imagine having someone like that speak into your life daily. She's amazing."

The waiter finally returned with our food, placing our plates down in front of us.

"Any issues so far?"

I blessed the food, then threw a couple of fries into my mouth. "I mean, we definitely have some challenges when it comes to how we express ourselves. I'm more open, she's a little tough, which can cause us to bump heads, but overall, we're good."

She bit into her burger. "I'm really happy for you, bro. I haven't heard one bad thing about her."

We continued eating, discussing everything from world news to business. Things at Mocha Tea & Trends were going really well, and I knew Sahana had her eye on buying a few pieces of property. It was something we'd discussed in the past, to see if we could start flipping properties.

"Dad said he would help me with the first property," she said, finishing her soda. "He seems to be getting better, too. I'm happy about that."

"Thank God. I told him the other day he looked great. Just call me if he starts acting weird again. He needs to stay on top of his health."

I noticed how she shifted in her seat, then looked down at her empty plate.

"What?"

She slowly looked back up at me. "Okay. Listen, I'm not sure what's going on. I wasn't going to say anything because I know we both can overreact sometimes—"

THE ESSENCE OF HIS SOUL

"I knew he wasn't taking his meds like he said," I blurted.

She placed her hand on my arm. "Calm down. That's not it."

I relaxed my shoulders.

"For the last month or so, every time I come home, him and Mom are always whispering. If I come into the living room and they're talking, they quickly change subjects. I don't think it's anything, but...it just feels off."

I sat quietly, trying to think what would make them be so secretive. "I mean, other than Dad's health, what do you think they could be hiding?"

"Mom's health?"

I cocked my head to the side. "Maybe, but at some point, they would've said something by now. Neither one of our birthdays are coming up, so we know it's not a surprise."

She pushed her plate away and leaned forward on the bar. "I don't know if it's anything, but..."

I looked at her. When I realized what she was saying, I gasped. "You think it has something to do with that DM, don't you?"

She bit her bottom lip. "Maybe. Listen, I don't think our parents would lie, but all the whispering, jumping whenever I come into a room and changing the subject, something is definitely off."

I nodded. "Yeah, it is, and we're going to figure it out. Just stay cool for now. God's timing is always perfect."

* * *

ESSENCE ALMOST MADE me drop the bottle of wine I was opening. I told her to meet me on the rooftop of a private location, kind of sending her on a scavenger hunt so she could go shopping for the gifts I'd gotten her along the way. I sent her around in a limousine and made sure she felt safe as she FaceTimed me the whole time.

Now, she was walking toward me, looking like a golden goddess wrapped in the sun. I'd only gotten a few peeks of her dress through the phone, but now, the way the beautiful, one-strap dress laid against her umber skin was breathtaking. She barely had on makeup and, of course, her hair framed her face perfectly. I placed the bottle down and reached for her as she drew closer. Hugging her tightly, I grabbed the bag of gifts out of her hand and placed it on the table.

We shared a kiss that almost made me want to tear her out of her dress. Thank God for the promise we made. I stopped before things got too heavy.

"Wow," was all I could say as she stood back.

She tugged on my shirt. "Wow, yourself. You look scrumptious."

Sharing a laugh, I moved a few things around as we settled into our seats. I opened her bag of gifts.

"So, you found everything, I see."

Her hand flew to her chest. "I don't think I've ever had so much fun in my life. At first, I was pissed because you know how long it takes me to flat iron my hair, especially now that it's growing back like crazy. My edges were sweating as I was running around town, looking for this stuff." She laughed. "But it was worth it. Thank you, baby."

I rubbed her arm gently. "It was fun to put together and I'm happy you had fun. Your hair looks perfect," I said, tugging on it lightly.

"Listen, this half-Cuban and half-black hair gets frizzy at the first drop of water or exercise. Lesson number one through twenty that black men need to remember about a woman."

Laughing, I poured us both a glass of Merlot. "Well, I'll get your hair done every week if I need to. But if that's frizzy, then baby, I'll take it."

She blew me a kiss, then asked about my day. I filled her in on everything that happened with Sahana and waited for her reaction.

"Well, that's kind of unnerving," she said. "The fact that Sahana picked up on your parents' weird behavior and think it actually has something to do with the DM is scary, but wait, babe— let's play around with this idea. What if this girl is telling the truth? Does that mean she's broken some adoption agreement? Don't they usually seal the files or something? Does that mean your dad has an outside child?"

I cut my eyes at her.

"I'm just asking. You're the one considering that this might be true."

I took a deep breath. "I know, babe. I'm sorry. It's just wild. I mean, those honestly are the only two explanations, right?"

"Yeah. And then, there's the chance that she's lying."

I stood up to go grab our food, kissing her forehead softly. "Let's eat, then we can talk about something else for a while." I walked toward the door that led inside. "Besides, I have one more surprise."

She grinned as I disappeared inside. I ran down to the restaurant, then grabbed our food out of the oven. One of the benefits of being well connected was having friends who owned a little of everything. One of my friends from the Eagles owned the restaurant downstairs. I asked him last week if I could have it tonight, so I could use the rooftop and the chef. It was never cheap to have a restaurant close early to their regular diners just to rent it out for a few hours, but it was always worth it for someone like Essence. Grabbing our food, I carried it carefully back upstairs to the rooftop.

"Here you go, my lady."

She eyed the plate, then licked her lips. "This looks insane. I know you didn't make this."

"Dang, baby. You doubt me like that?"

She raised an eyebrow.

"Okay, okay. The chef made it before he left. He just showed me how to heat it up."

I sat back down and blessed the food. We dug in, sharing our delight every few bites and cracking jokes in between. It was great spending time with someone you loved, with no phones in sight to distract you. We started keeping our phones away ever since that night at her place we argued about Clayton.

"So, what's this last surprise?" she asked, finishing her last bite of food. "You've already given me so much, not to mention another five pounds because of this meal."

"You still look good," I said, winking. I looked at my watch. "It actually should be arriving in a few minutes. Grab your wineglass."

She grabbed it and I grabbed mine, then we walked over to the ledge where we could look out and see the beautiful skyscrapers and lights that lit up the Philly skyline.

"This is such a gorgeous view," she said.

After another minute, I looked up and saw the signal. "Okay, baby. You ready? Look up there."

Instantly, fireworks went off, left and right. I didn't want her to miss it, so I pulled out my phone to catch everything as more rockets shot up in the sky and spelled out, 'I love you, Essence'.

"Baby, you see that?" I asked excitedly.

I didn't hear anything. I turned around to see her crouched down, close to the ledge, with her ears covered. I dropped my glass of wine, glass shattering everywhere, then bent down beside her.

"Baby, what happened? Did one of the fireworks hit you or something?" I asked, checking her body intensely. I didn't see anything, but then again, she was still crouched down.

She was shaking like a leaf. The display was almost over, but I grabbed her around the waist, then picked her up and carried her inside. *What is going on?* I walked toward the front of the restaurant, where guests usually waited for their table. Sitting her down in one of the plush chairs, I sat across from her and pulled my chair close. Her hands were no longer over her ears, but she was still shaking and now, crying. I reached for her hand.

"This is the second time we've been together and a loud noise has made you react in a way that's really scaring me," I said softly. "What's going on?"

She tried to catch her breath, so I waited patiently. After a few minutes, she finally spoke, but she wouldn't look at me.

"I was in the ninth grade. We were at lunch when it happened."

She bit her bottom lip. I wasn't going to interrupt or ask questions. I needed to know what was bothering her.

"It was 1:16 p.m., to be exact," she continued. "At first, nobody knew why everyone who was on the other end of the lunchroom was screaming and running. We thought they were just playing around, but then, then I saw him. I saw him and the gun."

She wiped at her face. "He started shooting again, aiming for a few students. All I remember is three bodies dropping before one of my friends threw me under the lunchroom table and covered my body. I was in complete shock. I mean, you hear about it all the time, right? School shooting and everything gets shut down. I never imagined it happening to us..."

I stroked her hand gently. It all made sense.

"Finally, we made it to the bathroom when he went up to the

second floor. We heard more shooting, but we made it inside the girls' bathroom where we knew the window would open wide enough so we could squeeze through. We heard sirens as we ran into the bathroom, so somebody had already called the police, thank God."

She finally looked at me. "It was the worst day of my life. They said the shooting started around 1:16 p.m. and only lasted for twelve minutes, but I felt like it lasted for hours. I climbed through the window, and when my feet hit the ground, I remember thinking about what it would have been like for the school to notify my parents that I had been murdered."

"I'm sorry, baby. I'm so, so sorry that happened to you."

She lunged into my arms and I stroked her back as she cried. It was crazy to think how long she'd been holding that in.

"Why didn't you tell me? I could've been careful in the things I planned for you."

"To be honest, it's not something I share with people. Trish knows because she's like a sister, but that's really it. It's hard to talk about, and while I did go to therapy, there are just some scars that don't heal all the way."

"The noise that day at the shop..."

"Took me right back to that place."

I nodded in understanding, but there was something I didn't quite get.

"Baby, you're at concerts and loud venues quite a bit with your clients. How does that work?"

She took a deep breath, then pulled away from me. "I actually prayed that being in the music industry would help me overcome my fears, and in many ways, it has. There was a time I couldn't even stand next to a large speaker without jumping. I guess because music has a rhythm, it makes it easier for me to deal with loud noises concerning the business. But fireworks, unexpected loud noises, even sometimes car crashes, they all make me shut down."

That actually made a lot of sense. I was proud of her for even going into a noisy industry. I read somewhere before that music could go as loud as a hundred decibels.

"You're so brave," I said, rubbing her cheek.

She forced a smile. "Am I?"

I pulled her back into my arms. "You're always trying to be so tough, but you don't have to be with me. You're strong because that's just who you are. You don't have to prove anything to me or anyone."

"Thanks, babe," she said, sniffling.

I continued rubbing her back as we sat there in silence. It was amazing what some people dealt with. I never would've imagined it was a school shooting. One of the things I enjoyed about being in love was learning new things about Essence. However, I realized that the things that hurt her were also a part of that. Sadly, I didn't have an answer for everything and while I knew I didn't have to, there was a part of me that wanted to protect her from ever being hurt again.

Thirteen

ESSENCE

WE WERE WELL into the summer and we hadn't broken our flow yet. Today, we were hanging out in my studio and I was showing him a day in my work life. He'd been here a few times before, but he never really explored all the rooms or played around in the sound booth like most people who take tours do.

"Why did you choose these colors?" he asked, as we entered the recording studio again. I sat down at the soundboard. "They're nice together, just seems odd for a recording studio."

"Well, purple symbolizes royalty and burgundy makes me feel like I'm absorbed in the music when I'm here. It's one of those colors that just hugs you, you know?"

He leaned on the soundboard, then played with a few buttons. I showed him how to adjust the sound and tempo to a track by turning on a track I was working on with a local producer. He smiled when he realized how easy it was.

"So, when are you going to sing for me?" he asked.

Our eyes met. "Who said I can sing?"

"There's no way you write all these dope songs for other people, know how to arrange music the way you do, and not know how to sing." He leaned down so we were nose to nose. "So, let me hear it."

I smirked. Of course, I had a voice, but it wasn't anything too serious.

"First of all, there are plenty of producers and songwriters in the business that can't sing. Someone can have an ear for music and not know how to sing."

He spun my chair around until I was facing him again. "So, are you saying you can't sing?"

Shaking my head, I laughed. "You're so irking."

He grabbed my hands and led me to the booth. I stopped.

"No. I will sing right here, just a few lines of something I'm working on, but that's it. I'm not going in there."

He threw his hands up in surrender. "Okay, okay. No pressure."

I took a deep breath, then started singing a few lines of a song I'd written for Remi. She had more of a Neo-soul vibe than Winter, so the song fit her. It was about a woman who'd had miscarried a baby, but the metaphor was that the baby was love and she didn't handle it properly, so she ended up miscarrying. When I was done, Shane clapped.

"You really can sing. Don't downplay it."

I sat back down. "I mean, who didn't sing in the choir growing up? You're a PK. You know how it goes."

"Yeah, but Sister Lenora could barely sing, and please don't tell Sister Bertha she can't have her Sunday solo."

We cracked up, because it was true. Most people in the choir couldn't sing. There were a few promising voices, but most of the time, Sister Bertha and Sister Lenora got their way because nobody wanted to deal with the foolishness. When we were done laughing, he looked at me.

He grabbed my hand and kissed it. "The more I learn about you, the more I admire about you."

I pulled the other chair closer to me and patted the seat. "Join me. Let's see if we can make some music together. Just for fun."

"I like the music we've been making lately. It's got a pretty dope vibe."

I kissed him. "Then let's make some more."

* * *

I MOVED to the side as Extra interviewed Winter about her upcoming release. Happy to see all of my artists were on the red carpet tonight, I turned to make small talk with a few celebrities standing nearby. The lights were so bright, I had to shield my eyes just to see who was coming up next on the step and repeat. The crowd standing behind the barricades grew louder as Cyn, a rising actress, stepped up.

I smiled, appreciating all the love Black people were getting tonight. It was a beautiful night in New York for the Black Women in Music and Hollywood Honoree event, which launched a few years ago and, since then, had been bringing out the best and brightest in Hollywood.

"Hey, Boss Lady," Winter said, lightly grabbing my arm. "This is so much fun. I can't believe I'm even here."

"I told you when you signed, I would make sure you had access and exposure. You need to be at events like this. Shows you what you can achieve."

She nodded. "Are you upset you weren't nominated for anything?"

I shook my head. "Not at all. I've only been at this for almost six years, and while some may think I'm supposed to have an award by now, there are so many black women who've been killing it longer than me. My time will come."

"That's why I love having you as a manager and being signed to your label. Everything is done with patience and excellence. I really admire you and Trish." She looked around. "Speaking of, where is she?"

"She's coming with her date, so they should be here soon."

Her eyes landed on the step and repeat. "Speaking of dates, I was just about to ask where yours was, but I see he wanted to make an entrance."

I turned just in time to see Shane turn toward a few cameramen. He looked like a bottle of fine wine in the two-piece Armani suit he'd picked out for tonight. It was a nice, orange suit that laid against his skin perfectly, and for a second, I was jealous of the suit. His goatee was nicely trimmed, along with his low-cut Caesar. He smiled for a few more pictures, then made his way to the end of the step and repeat. I was about to make my way toward him when his eyes landed on me and he walked toward me.

"You guys didn't want to come together?" Winter asked.

I never took my eyes off him. "We wanted to surprise everyone. You know the blogs are talking, and while we're public, we don't want them thinking they know our every move."

We originally planned to go public tonight, but once Shane read my blog post I was waiting to publish, we felt peace with letting that be our official public announcement. That was almost two months ago, and it had served us well.

Before he fully reached me, he had his arm out and around my waist. He pulled me into him and kissed me lightly on my lips. Without skipping a beat, I kissed him again and melted into his arms. We must've been hugging for a long time because Winter tapped me on the shoulder.

"Guys, you're definitely giving them what they want right now," she said.

We pulled back from each other and noticed that many of the cameras that weren't with the step and repeat press team were on us. Instead of shying away, we posed and had fun, throwing up the peace sign in every photo and making funny faces. It was our first big event together and I couldn't be happier that we could finally let our hair down.

"You look gorgeous, as always," he whispered in my ear. "I couldn't wait to get to you."

"You walked on that red carpet like you owned the place," I said, looking into his eyes. "And to be honest, tonight, you got it, baby."

As we continued flirting with each other, a reporter from Bossip strolled over to us.

"So, is this the first public lover's debut from Essence Taylor and Shane Bishop? I don't know, guys, let's ask them now."

We faced her as she thrust the microphone in my face. "How does it feel to be official with the hottest basketball player in the game?"

I frowned. Before I could respond, Shane stepped in. "You mean, how does it feel for me to have one of the most beautiful women in the world on my arm tonight? It feels special."

He winked at me as I finally forced a smile on my face. I was used to the cameras and interviews, but this was definitely new for me. Dixon wasn't a high-profile person, so keeping people out of my business was a lot easier. I grabbed Shane's hand as he continued talking.

"How long has it been officially?" the reporter asked.

"We've been together about four months," he said. "We just wanted to build privately and let our fans know when we were ready, but it looks like you guys took care of that for us."

I chuckled at his sarcasm.

"Now, you know we like being the ones with the exclusive. To be honest, I was surprised to see you settled down after everything that happened with Rayna. Have you heard from her?"

Shane cleared his throat. Now it was time for me to step in. "We don't focus on our past. We have a beautiful future together and we're looking forward to seeing how God uses us."

I felt my father's voice in that last line, which made me smile. Usually, whenever you mentioned God, people got the message and moved on.

"Well, Bossip family, you heard it here first. The two lovebirds have declared their love for the first time together, right here at the Black Women in Music and Hollywood Honoree Event. David, back to you."

Before she could say anything else, Shane whisked me away. I looked for Winter and saw her chatting with a couple of people over on the other side of the carpet. Finally able to catch a breath, I looked up at Shane as we stood near the entrance of the venue. Everyone would be headed inside in a few.

"You were amazing back there," I said. "I love how protective you were."

"Nobody's going to mess with my woman with their messiness." He kissed my cheek.

"Well, Mr. Bishop, since we're giving them what they want tonight, let's get on that step and repeat and really give them the business."

He grabbed my hand as we made our way over. "I thought you'd never ask."

* * *

MY FEET WERE ON FIRE, and I couldn't find Shane. We decided on Cyn's after party since she had invited us personally. I was glad we'd gotten two rooms at the Hilton here in New York because driving back to Philly tonight would've never happened. I wasn't drinking tonight and had no plans on it, but I knew Shane had had a few drinks and he would definitely be ready to crash. I took a seat on one of the couches they had in the center of the room. I texted Shane and relaxed against the couch. The woman sitting near me smiled, then turned her attention to me.

"You're Essence Taylor, right?"

Surprised, I reached out my hand to her. "Yes, nice to meet you. What's your name?"

"Zuri Peoples. I'm actually here as a plus one."

"Most of the plus ones are the real MVPs," I said.

"Well, I appreciate that. I've been following your new artist, Winter. I'm actually looking forward to her album."

As we continued talking, I felt my phone buzzing in my bag. I excused myself, then checked the message. Great. Shane said he'd be ready to go in twenty minutes.

"I'm actually getting ready to head out, but it was nice speaking with you."

"Thank you for taking the time. So many people here are kind of uppity, but you were certainly a breath of fresh air."

Smiling, I waved and walked over to the cocktail area where he wanted us to meet. As I neared it, I looked over toward the section, off to the side. I squinted to be sure I wasn't tripping. It was definitely Shane. With a woman. I walked a little closer, but not enough that they would see me. Hiding behind the drape that separated the two areas, I listened intently.

"You can move, or I can have you moved," he said.

What is going on?

"Oh, lighten up. I know you're dating that music chick. I was just looking to have some fun."

My nostrils flared as I waited for his response.

"Fun? You come over here pretending to be interested in helping me secure a book deal, then start flirting with me? If the roles were reversed, you'd be screaming sexual harassment."

I heard some movement. He must've been trying to walk around her.

"Actually, I wouldn't," she said with a laugh.

I was trying hard not to knock this heifer down.

"Lady, I'm trying not to embarrass you and make a scene, but I will to protect me and mine. Now, I'm going to ask you one last time. Move."

Beaming with pride, I slowly tiptoed away from the drape and headed toward the cocktail area. I had nothing to worry about when it came to my man. Women were going to try him, that was for certain, but as long as he put them in their place, I wouldn't have to.

* * *

FINALLY, in my hotel room, I laid on my bed, kicking my shoes off, and slowly removed my dress. I was careful not to rip it, since I was returning it to my stylist. Shane and I talked in the lobby before coming up. I didn't tell him I'd heard everything, and he didn't bring it up. There was no need. We just chatted about the night, talking about who looked great and who looked a mess. We'd been careful to maintain our boundaries, so talking in the lobby was the best thing to do.

He'd gotten me a room on the same floor as him, but several doors down. Shoot, I was tempted to go to his room with the way he looked tonight. Being abstinent wasn't easy, especially when I thought about the guys who had been a waste of my time. Over the last four months, we'd made out a few times and had to add more boundaries just to make sure we kept our word to God.

As I continued getting comfortable, I shot Trish a text. She'd shown up five minutes before everyone went in, giving us a chance to take photos on the carpet, along with Maurice and Shane taking a few. We were all going to hang out together soon.

I wanted to run a bath, but it was almost two in the morning. I would just crash, then take a nice, long bath tomorrow morning. Grabbing my phone, I headed to the bathroom to at least take care of my personal business. I opened up my Instagram app, posting a few pictures to my stories. Just when I was about to close the app, I saw I had a few messages. I opened the first one.

Message 1: Girl, I don't mean to tell you this, but Shane and I were together the other night. I think you had a meeting with some producer. I just wanted to let you know that your man ain't faithful.

Message 2: Hey love. I don't mean to burst your bubble, but Shane and my sister are dating. He was just with her last week.

I shook my head. There were at least two more like it. I closed my eyes, trying to keep the room from spinning. I wasn't tripping because I knew they weren't true. I just hated that this came with the territory. I trusted Shane. Not just because of what I witnessed tonight, but because we were pretty much always together, and I knew he wouldn't do me like that. Until he showed me otherwise, all these girls could go to hell.

I deleted the messages, blocking at least six people in the process. Then, I saw another one. This one was from a guy. One I thought I'd blocked years ago.

Hey, beautiful. Never saw you as the baller type. I pray he's treating you right. Any chance we can link up soon?

I went to his page and realized why he'd been able to get through. He had a new Instagram page. *Well, Dixon, you can create all the pages you want. I'll just keep blocking them, too.* I laid my phone face down on the sink and looked up at the ceiling.

"God, I know You blessed me with this man and I'm not going to run when the enemy strikes. Help us both to block out the noise and stay focused on You and each other, but I do ask You to please keep these women on a leash and these exes out of our way. In Jesus's name, Amen."

Fourteen

SHANE

I WAS FINISHING up my morning run down Kelly Drive. It had been a week since the honoree event, and it felt like I was on cloud nine. I had to admit, when Essence showed me the DMs, I was livid. I remember how hard my leg shook in the lobby as we talked. She calmed me down, putting my heart at ease when she told me she wasn't worried about them. It seemed like whenever the enemy tried to cause tension between us through other people, we were able to get right back on track, block the offender, and keep it moving.

Yesterday, we fasted together. This was my first time fasting with someone I was in a relationship with, and when we were done, to have a praying woman holding you down had a whole new meaning to it. This morning, we read a few devotions together and prayed. While I'd seen this example growing up, I hadn't experienced it on my own. My father told me all the time that having a woman you connected with spiritually was the best thing about a relationship. Now, I knew why.

Since I only had two months before training camp, we were going to spend as much of the summer together as possible. I worried often about how I would keep up with our groove, but Essence kept telling me not to stress. "If Grant Hill could play for Orlando while Tamia was living in Canada, we certainly can work this out," she'd say. Her optimism balanced out my overthinking, which I needed.

I focused back on the final stretch of my run. Finally, I came to a stop, leaning on the railing near me. I was catching my breath when my phone went off.

Smiling, I checked the notification, thinking it was my baby. When I saw the email notification, I opened my email.

"Hi, Shane. It took me forever to track down your personal email. I know you probably wish I would leave you alone, but we're both innocent in all of this and I just want to meet my brother. My mother is upset about this, but I don't care. It's not fair that we're the ones who have to pay for our parents' mistake. I promise you I'm not lying. Can we at least meet? If you don't believe me from the evidence I'll show you, then I promise to go away and never bother you again. I'll even sign something saying I won't. Please hear me out. Casey."

If she didn't have my attention before, she had it now. First of all, this girl must be pretty good with investigating because my personal email couldn't be guessed easily, and only close family and friends had it. I know they wouldn't give it out. Second, the whole "my mother is upset about this" made the hairs on my neck stand up. If she was telling the truth, this woman was willing to upset her own mother to prove what she knew was true. It could all be a sham, but did it hurt to meet with her?

I could call my security guy to go with me. I only used him when we traveled internationally or did NBA off-season events. I could even ask Essence to go, just in case this girl was crazy. With those two there, she couldn't try but so much. I would entertain her little story, and if she turned out to be crazy and this was about money, I'd have her arrested on the spot and press charges. Simple as that.

If it's that simple, why do you feel like she might be telling the truth?

I tried to silence my thoughts, but this thing had been gnawing at me. When I blocked her on Instagram, I thought it was over. Now, I was getting ready to open up a can of worms that could change my life forever.

* * *

THE ESSENCE OF HIS SOUL

I NODDED AT NICK, my bodyguard, who was sitting at the high counter of the coffee shop near the window, about fifty feet from where we sat. Essence and I were sitting at a table, drinking coffee. My leg shook like crazy. Essence placed her hand on my knee, calming me down. I checked my phone for the eighth time, then looked outside to see if she was coming. She had sent me a picture of herself. Other than the deep brown eyes, I saw no resemblance.

"She'll be here, babe. I know it's hard, but relax."

"How can I? What if she's telling the truth?"

Essence swallowed, but didn't respond. When I'd first gotten the DM, she was so adamant that it was a lie. Now, we both weren't so sure. We opened in two hours and I didn't want anyone here when this went down. I chose seven in the morning for that very reason. Just when I was about to check my phone again, Nick hollered, "Incoming!"

I looked and it was her. He stood up and unlocked the door as she shuffled inside. He locked it back up, then pointed to her bag.

"I need to check your bag."

Casey frowned, then looked over at me. Finally, she handed him the bag. He checked it, then lightly patted her down.

"I guess you can't be too careful these days," she said, nearing our table.

Essence gasped. It was enough reaction for both of us. The picture she sent must've been pretty old because, as this girl got closer, there was no way I could deny the resemblance. Sahana looked like our father and I always felt like I looked like our mother. Casey and I definitely shared the same skin tone, eyes, and even the cheekbone structure. I shook my head. None of this made sense.

"Hi. Nice to meet you both," she said, sitting down. "I don't want to waste your time, so I'll get straight to it."

She swallowed, looked at Essence, then turned her attention back to me. "This isn't about money or anything. I'm not some crazed stalker. I promise."

She stared into my eyes.

"I just don't see how you can be my sister. My parents have been together for almost thirty-three years and my mother has never mentioned a child she had prior to meeting my father, which would have to be the case, right? Were you put up for adoption or something?"

I saw her swallow. She looked down at her hands that were resting on the table, then back at me.

"How old are you?" Essence asked.

"I'm thirty-one."

"Okay," I said. "Then this really makes no sense."

"Babe, let her explain."

I relaxed under Essence's touch.

"You said you had evidence?" Essence continued.

"There's really no easy way to say this, Shane. I'm not here to break up anyone's family, but your mother isn't my mother."

I shook my head. "So, you're saying my father is your father? You tryna say he cheated on my mom?"

She reached in her bag and pulled out an envelope. "I promise these aren't doctored photos."

She slid them across the table. I grabbed the envelope and opened it. There were pictures inside. As I pulled them out, my mouth fell open. It was my mother, but the man in the picture wasn't my father.

"Who's this man?" I asked, flipping through the pictures quickly. There were some of them at the park. Others of them sitting on a car. There were even some of them hugged up. He certainly wasn't a relative.

"That's Mason Kirkwood. My father."

I shook my head. "This doesn't make sense. Why was he with my mother? When were these taken?"

Essence grabbed one of the photos and turned it over. "It says March 1992."

"Wait. What?"

I looked at the back of the rest of the photos. I was born in February 1993. There was no way.

"Casey, please explain this. What is going on?" I pleaded.

"My parents were married for three years before my father met your mother. My mother knew something was going on, so she hired a private investigator. She knew something was off because he worked from home as an engineer. All of a sudden, work trips came out of nowhere and he was spending more and more time out of the house. These are the photos the private investigator gave her."

Essence looked through the photos now. I stared at Casey, trying to piece together what she was telling me. My throat was in my stomach because this could only mean one thing.

"These aren't all of them, but I'm not trying to hurt you," Casey continued. "The others were a bit more explicit."

"Are you trying to tell us that Mason Kirkwood is Shane's father?" Essence finally asked.

Casey looked at her, then at me. Tears filled her eyes as she nodded slowly. I looked at her face, searching for a lie somewhere, but the pictures told it all.

After a few minutes, I felt my heartbeat returning to normal.

"Where is he now?" I asked, finally able to speak.

"He died in a fire when I was four. So, I believe you were two at the time."

"That's why this was kept so quiet," Essence said.

"How did you figure all of this out? And why now?" I asked, leaning on the table.

"When our father died, I didn't know anything about another child, of course. I grew up like any other kid, being raised in a single-parent home. But one day, I went upstairs to our attic to find some of my father's old pictures for a gift for my mother. I guess she forgot to lock those up because I found them. I hid them for like a week before I asked her about them, especially since there were pics clearly showing they were together intimately."

I shifted in my seat. "How did I come up?"

"Wait... are you telling me your mother knew your father had another child all this time?" Essence asked, her face contorted.

Casey nodded. "At first, my mother only told me about the affair. But then, there were a few pictures of your mother pregnant. I wanted to know why she continued to have your mother investigated if they had broken up. That's when she told me he refused to not have anything to do with the baby's life. I knew."

I fell back against the seat. "So, my mother had an affair with a married man and got pregnant by him? How do you or your mother know that Lawrence Bishop isn't my real father? My mother clearly was intimate with both of them."

Casey reached in her bag again. "Are you sure you want to see this?"

"You've already disrupted my life. Why hold back now?"

I saw the hurt look on her face when I said that, but I didn't care. Somebody had to pay for the way I felt, and since she decided to open up pandora's box, it would be her. For now.

She pulled out a piece of paper that looked like it had been run over by a truck a hundred times. It was definitely worn out and ripped on the edges. She handed it to me. I grabbed it and opened it up. I squinted to read the information, but the most important line was clear as day.

STATEMENT OF RESULTS: *The alleged father cannot be excluded as the biological father of the tested child. Based on the analysis of STR loci listed above, the probability of paternity is 99.9999999%.*

I LOOKED at the top and there was Mason's name as the alleged father and mine as the alleged child.

"Why did your mother keep this?" Essence asked.

"I asked her the same thing. She said she always wanted him to remember how he'd betrayed her. I think she thought about confronting your mother a few times and she didn't want her to deny the truth. So, she kept the photos and the test he brought home to her."

Essence looked at me, then rubbed the back of my head gently. "I'm sorry, baby. This is heavy, but Casey isn't lying."

I knew she wasn't. Everything was laying right here.

"My mother told me she made him get the test done because of the circumstances. I think your mother wanted it to be Mr. Bishop's. It would obviously help them move past the situation easier."

I wiped the tears that streamed down my face away. "I can't believe they lied to me. For almost thirty years, they've been lying to me!"

Essence grabbed my face. "I know, baby, I know." She looked at Casey again. "So, what do you want?"

"Honestly, I just want a relationship with my brother. This has nothing to do with fame or money. I've been by myself all my life and I really just want a relationship."

"You do realize he's going to need some time, right?"

Casey nodded. "Of course. I wouldn't expect anything less, and even if you decide to say no, I get that, too. I just felt betrayed that my mother didn't tell me my father had another child."

"You feel betrayed?" I huffed. "I can't believe this. All this time, I kept thinking my mother must've lied to all of us when, in reality, they both lied to me. My father isn't my father."

I tried to control my shaking, but I couldn't. I was beyond angry. As bad as I wanted to, there was no way I would be going to see my parents tonight. I would have to confront them tomorrow or Sunday.

"Listen, he has your number and information. Let him sort this out, then he'll reach out," Essence said. "In the meantime, I think it's best you respect his privacy."

"I promised I would. I can sign anything saying I won't take this to the press or whatever. I'm not like that. I just... I just didn't think it was right."

Essence reached for her hand. "I get it. He's not angry at you. It's just a lot to absorb and doing it with the request you've made is a lot right now."

She looked at the pictures. "Do you want to hold on to that and the DNA test?"

I nodded. "Yeah," I said, grabbing them and handing them to Essence so she could put them in her bag. "But I have one more question. You said something about you tried to get in touch with me through my parents. What happened there?"

My mind raced back to Sahana, mentioning their weird behavior and the whispering.

"I reached out to your mom at first, against my mother's wishes. I sent her an email to her church email address, asking if we could talk. I didn't say what it was about because I knew she wouldn't call. When she called me, I told her everything, but I assured her this wasn't about anything other than wanting to meet you. She knew I was telling the truth because I told her details about my father that only a child would know. Once she said she wouldn't put me in touch with you, that was it."

I took a deep breath, then reached for Casey's hand. "You sound like you're a genuine person who just wanted the truth. I can appreciate that. But like my baby said, please don't reach out again. I'll reach out when I'm ready."

She grabbed her bag and stood up. "No problem. I'm really sorry about all this. I pray the healing can begin."

She headed to the door and Nick let her out. I looked at Essence. Before I could speak, she had me in her arms. I thought losing the season was the worst thing that could happen this year. Right now, I felt like I'd lost my whole family with just one conversation.

Fifteen

ESSENCE

TWO DAYS HAD PASSED since Shane and I sat with Casey and he still hadn't talked to his parents. As I watched him resting on my couch, I thought about all the reasons why they would allow something like this to get out of hand. Once Casey started contacting them, they should've been the first to say something, so I understood Shane's point of view. We knew our parents weren't perfect, but there were just some things that shouldn't happen.

I stood up to head into the kitchen to make myself a snack. I had a craving for Doritos, but I opted for something healthier. I'd been watching my weight over the last few weeks. I was pretty healthy, but I noticed my jeans felt a little snug. Shane didn't think it was an issue. I smiled as I stuffed a spoonful of chia pudding into my mouth. Sitting on the kitchen counter, I watched him stir in his sleep. I took slower bites as my mind whirled about his next steps.

Once I was done, I cleaned up the kitchen, then headed to the patio with my phone. Grateful for the beautiful, summer day, I closed the patio door behind me and sat down. Admiring the few potted plants I had sitting around the deck's edge, I smiled. I was hardly a green thumb, but Trader Joe's always made me buy flowers and plants. As I stared at them, I wondered why things like this happened to decent people. Shane wasn't perfect, but he tried to honor his parents and he certainly had integrity.

I hadn't been able to shake the heaviness that rested on my heart. I felt like it was happening to me. The hardest part was I needed encouragement myself because I didn't know what to do. I was running out of words of encouragement and even my prayers were becoming redundant. But of course, I couldn't tell anyone, and I wouldn't.

"God, I know this isn't too big for You, but the last forty-eight hours have been frustrating to say the least. Help me be there for him the best I can. I've never wanted to help someone so bad in my life."

I looked down at my phone. Trish had texted me. I still hadn't given her an answer about tonight. I'd only told her I had a personal family matter to deal with and that I may not attend tonight's event. At the time I told her, it was a maybe, but the heavier I felt, the more I was sure I wouldn't go. I needed to let her know.

Hey, sis. Thanks for your patience. Yes, if you can stand in tonight for me, I would appreciate it. I will fill you in when I can, but for now, nobody is dying. Love you.

Without waiting for her reply, I stood up and looked up at the sky. The sun was trying to come out from behind the clouds a little bit more. My mood hardly matched the beauty of the day, but I hoped the clouds would pass soon enough.

* * *

"THANK YOU, BABY," he said, grabbing the bowl of spaghetti and dipping some on his plate.

I'd made a last-minute meal once I realized we'd be staying inside all day. We hadn't made any official plans, but I thought he would want to get out and breathe a little.

"I can't believe I slept all day," he continued. "Sorry about that."

I bit into my garlic bread. "No need. Don't ever apologize for getting rest. You needed it."

"What did you do all day while I slept?"

"Honestly, just prayed and read the word. It's hard to focus when something like this hits close to home, ya know?"

He nodded. "Tell me about it. I'm thinking about training camp and how in the world I'll be able to focus."

I didn't want to upset him, but I had to ask. "Baby, training camp is over a month away. There's a lot more that needs to happen before then."

He stopped chewing. "I know I have to talk to them. It's not like I won't. I just need to figure out how I want to address it."

I relaxed my shoulders. I knew he would talk to his parents eventually, I just didn't want him to hold off much longer. They still needed to explain their side.

"I did tell Sahana I had something I needed to talk to our parents about and I needed her there with me."

I sat back against the chair. "You don't want me to go?"

He looked at me. "Babe, I think it's best I address this on my own. This is embarrassing for my parents, and although you've met them, I don't want them to feel anymore embarrassed."

I swallowed. That was a blow to my ego. We'd had dinner with his parents several times and even hung out at the movies once. He'd met my mom, but still hadn't met my dad, namely because my father was being a jerk. I thought we were at the place where if it concerned family, family showed up to support.

He reached for my hand. "I don't want you to feel like I'm pushing you away, but I really think it's going to be a lot with Sahana and I there. A third person will just add more anxiety."

I nodded slowly. "I get it," I said, removing my hand from under his. I quickly took a few sips of my wine.

He dropped his fork. "I don't like that. What's up? I can feel you don't like what I just said."

I pushed back from the table and walked to the sink. With my back to him, I responded, "It's fine, Shane. I get it. I shouldn't have assumed you would ask me to go with you."

I heard him push his chair back. I felt him walking up behind me. He wrapped me in his arms. As much as I wanted to fight it, I allowed my head to rest against his chest.

"I feel horrible making this about me. You have to do what's best for you and your parents."

"But I get it. You've been holding me down the last couple of days and now, you feel like I'm excluding you from the process."

I slowly turned to face him. "It's okay. I think I'm just used to being your ace boon."

He smiled, then kissed my forehead. "That hasn't changed." He placed his finger under my chin. "I love you."

I kissed him gently. "I love you."

He led me back over to the table. "Besides, I don't think you want to see that side of me. It's not going to be pretty. At all."

I forced a smile. He had put my heart at ease, but it didn't change that I wanted to be there for him physically. I just accepted I couldn't.

"Tomorrow. I'm doing it tomorrow," he blurted.

I didn't say anything.

"I figured today would've been messy, with it being Sunday. I know my father preached today."

"Makes sense. To be honest, the day doesn't matter. The result won't change as far as emotions."

He shrugged. "Yeah, but it made more sense to me."

I grabbed the salad and placed some on my plate. "Did you tell Sahana anything?"

He shook his head. "She's going to meet me at my place in the morning. Then we'll head to our parents."

I dug into my salad, letting him share his heart without interruption for the rest of the meal. Finally, we were on dessert, which was just small pudding tarts I grabbed from the market.

"Babe, I forgot. Didn't you have something to do tonight?" he asked.

I licked the pudding off my spoon. "I asked Trish to step in so I could be here with you tonight."

He stopped chewing. "Wait... you canceled for me?"

I looked down at my tart, then back at him. Maybe that was why I had felt some kind of way about him not wanting me to go with him to confront his parents. I had never canceled anything for a man before. The only time I'd ever done it was when my father had an emergency surgery, and even then, I was back to working once he woke up from surgery.

"Yeah. It's no big deal."

He grabbed my hand before I could take another bite of my tart. "It's a big deal to me."

He winked and my heart leaped. I smiled, blushing like crazy. He noticed. That meant something to me.

* * *

LATER THAT NIGHT, I called my mom. I wrestled with it all day, but I needed prayer.

"Hey, Baby Girl. What's going on?"

I broke down the second I heard her voice.

"Baby, what is it? Where are you?"

"I'm okay. I just need you to pray for me. I really don't know what to do," I whimpered into the phone.

"What's wrong? Tell me what it is."

"I can't. It's Shane's issue, not mine. But I need to know, when Dad had his hardest problem in life, how did you help him get through it?"

I heard her breathing. "Baby, that's a loaded question, but I got an answer. Let's pray first."

I closed my eyes as my mother went into prayer warrior mode. As she prayed, I felt the weight lift off my shoulders. This was what I needed. Now, I just hoped the feeling I felt now would last.

Sixteen

SHANE

AS I MOUNTED the steps to my parents' front door, my shoes felt like they had rocks in them. Sahana walked slowly beside me. I could tell by the solemn look on her face, she was still processing everything I'd told her. If it wasn't for the DNA test results and pictures, she wouldn't have believed me. I had to show the results for her to believe me. I swallowed and took out my key. All of a sudden, I felt sick. This key didn't have the same meaning. I wanted to knock because I didn't feel like family.

I texted my mom and told her we were coming by. It was close to dinnertime and I smelled the cornbread as I opened the door. Sahana grabbed my free hand as I pushed the door all the way open. I squeezed her shaking hand and pulled her inside. We took our shoes off by the door and made our way inside. I could tell by the jazz music that played that my parents were probably in the living room, dancing. It was their thing. We turned the corner to the living room and there they were, my father dipping my mother back.

"Hey, Son," my father said, laughing. "You see your old man still got it."

I nodded, trying not to jump right into the conversation I needed to have. "Hey."

Saying, 'hey, Pop' didn't feel right. I barely wanted to say, 'hey, Mom'.

My mother turned down the music as we fully entered the living room.

"There are my babies," she said, walking over. "Today must be special. We've got both our children with us at the same time without having to compete with their busy schedules." She looked at my dad. "They must want something," she teased.

I remained silent. Sahana forced a smile.

"Hey, Dad," she said, hugging him tightly. I winced.

I wrapped my mom in the best hug I could, but pulled away quickly. The tears were already brewing.

"Everything okay?" she asked.

I nodded. I knew if I spoke right now, it wouldn't be good. I needed to get my bearings together.

"So, what's for dinner?" Sahana asked.

"I made beef ribs, since I know that's your favorite, Son," my father said. "Your mom made some mac and cheese and yams. I made the greens. We need a veggie in there somewhere."

I glared at him. "Should you even be eating ribs?"

My concern for his health was still evident. I didn't want anything to happen to him.

"It's just one meal. I've been doing good, haven't I, Shandra?" he asked, turning to my mom.

"He's been doing okay. I would say a seven on a scale of one to ten."

She looked at me, then turned her attention to Sahana. "So, Honey, you've been coming home later and later these days. Catch us up on how things are going at the firm."

As Sahana caught our parents up on her work at the law firm, I pulled out my phone. My mother had a no-phone policy when we were spending time together, but I wanted to have my evidence ready.

"Son, is everything okay? You don't seem like yourself," my dad said.

I took a deep breath, then looked at Sahana. She shrugged.

My mom leaned forward. "Okay, what's up, you guys? What's all this morse code between you two?"

I looked at her. "What's all the morse code between us? I thought it was you two that were sharing morse codes over the last few months. At least, that's what Sahana tells me. All the whispering and stuff around the house."

Confusion fell on my mother's face. My father sat up. "Sahana, what whispering?"

She looked down at her hands. "Whenever I come home or when I'm walking around the house, you guys have been acting a little weird lately and I can tell you're changing the subject when I walk into a room."

My mother laughed nervously. "Oh, that. Your father's been trying to keep you children out of his health business for a long time. We thought he might need surgery and we just didn't want to scare you. You know how he is."

I felt my jaw clenching. Even now, they weren't willing to be honest.

"That's not what Casey Kirkwood is saying," I said.

No more beating around the bush.

I saw the color drain from my mother's face as she gripped my father's wrist. He sat there, frozen in place.

"Who's Casey Kirkwood, Mom? Dad?"

Sahana shifted in her seat. I saw her wipe a tear from her eye. I hated that this was hurting her, but we needed answers. The room was silent, except for Sahana's sniffles.

I placed my phone down on the table with one of the pictures of my mother and Mason displayed on it. Then, I changed the image to the one I took of the DNA test results.

"You have something you need to tell me?"

The timer went off in the kitchen. I smelled the barbecue sauce from the ribs. Sadly, the taste in my mouth was more reminiscent of vomit.

"I'll turn the oven off," Sahana said softly, heading into the kitchen.

I stared at my parents, waiting for them to speak. The tears that rolled down my mother's cheeks answered my question. Any doubts I had were erased with their silence and her crying.

"Son—"

"Don't call me that!" I yelled, slamming my hand on the coffee table. "Enough with the lies."

My father's eyes widened. I had never yelled at him in my life.

"Calm down, bro," Sahana said, coming back into the living room and resting her hand on my shoulder. "Mom, Dad, please. Just tell us the truth."

My mother looked down at my phone, then picked it up. The phone shook in her hands. "I can't believe she reached out to you."

"That's what you have to say?"

My father looked at me. "This isn't easy for us."

"Not easy for me, either," I said.

After a few more minutes of staring at the phone, my mother sat back and started speaking.

"I never meant to fall in love with another man. Your father was giving me the world and I couldn't have asked for a better man. Mason was an accident."

"Was I?" I blurted.

She looked at me, sitting up. "No. Absolutely not. I wanted you from the moment I found out I was pregnant."

She reached for my hand, but I backed away.

"So, what happened?"

She took a deep breath. "Your father and I hit a rough patch. Instead of telling him how I felt, I ran to the arms of another man. I met Mason at a church event. We didn't exchange numbers or anything because we were both married. It started off with us just meeting one another once a week at a small diner in South Philly. It was innocent at first. Just someone to talk to."

She paused, then looked at my father. He wouldn't take his eyes off me.

"Then it got more serious and we started having an affair. We thought we would only sleep together a few times, but we couldn't stop. Eventually, your father caught wind of it, and I cut it off. He confronted Mason and threatened to tell his wife, so we stopped. But by then, I was already pregnant."

She wiped her face with the back of her hand. My father grabbed her other hand, stroking it as she continued.

"I prayed and hoped it was your father's, but deep down, I knew it wasn't. We waited until you were born to have the DNA test and that's when we knew for sure."

While I had heard the story from Casey and had repeated it to Sahana, hearing it from the horse's mouth was more devastating than I had anticipated. I had to blink several times to clear the tears from my eyes.

"And you knew all this time and just went along with it, huh?" I said, my eyes landing on my father. "Why?"

"Because you needed a father, and I loved your mother. I accepted she made a mistake, and I knew his wife wouldn't make it easy for him to be present in your life. We got the test so we would know, but we always knew we would raise you as our own. She was happy with that because she didn't want her family broken up."

"So, you raised another man's child as your own, not thinking for once that I should know the truth?"

My father shrugged. "I know this sounds harsh, but why? Especially once Mason died, there was no point in digging up buried stuff."

Sahana jumped in. "But Dad, it wasn't buried. Did you guys even consider that at some point, his wife or even anyone else who knew the truth might come forward? What about once Shane got drafted? Did it ever occur to you that someone might try to extort him for money?"

My mother cleared her throat. "Is that what Casey is doing?"

I shook my head. "No. But that doesn't matter. Were you ever going to tell me?"

My father looked down at his feet, and my mother bit her bottom lip. My heart sank as I realized the truth. They were content living a lie and had no plans to come clean. I stood up.

"I gotta get out of here," I said, heading to the door.

"Son, wait. Please," I heard my mother say.

She rushed over to me, standing in front of me. "You mean the world to me. I wanted to make it right, but when Mason died, we knew you would never be able to meet him, so we thought it was best to just move on."

I smirked. "Best for who? Me? Sahana? Casey? What about Samuel? I mean, all these years, I've been feeling guilty about my brother's death and thinking I could've been a better big brother. Yet, my parents were the ones who could've been better parents."

"We never blamed you for that."

Now, I really had to go. "Oh, because you're the perfect Christian parents, right? I saw the looks throughout my childhood. I saw the disdain and I definitely heard the remarks when family and friends continued sending over their condolences. You may not have said it directly, but I felt it."

Our family barely talked about Samuel, but when we did, you felt the room shift. I felt heavier than I did when we first arrived. I finished putting on my sneakers, then grabbed the doorknob.

"Son, please don't leave like this. Please," my father said, coming up behind me.

I whirled around. "You can't sow seeds like this and not deal with the consequences." I turned back to leave. "I need space. Sahana, I'll call you later."

I left without looking back. Once I was in my truck, I banged my hands against the steering wheel. For the next five minutes, I cursed and shouted. Why was God letting this happen? Why now?

* * *

I PULLED up at Essence's and turned my truck off. I had a key to her place, but I called her, anyway. We had only talked this morning when she prayed over me.

"Baby, I've been waiting for you to call. How did it go?" she asked as soon as she picked up.

"I'm here," was all I said.

"Well, come up."

She hung up. I waited in the truck for a few more minutes, then slowly got out. Once the doorman let me by, I made my way up to her condo and knocked.

"Why didn't you use your key?" she asked, opening the door.

Her smile quickly faded as I fell into her arms.

"It's okay. It's okay," she said.

She led me over to her couch and let me weep in her arms. I held onto her waist tightly, barely able to speak.

"It was horrible," I said finally.

"You have to promise me, Essence, that you'll always be honest with me. I can't take any more lies."

My head was in her lap, and she stroked the side of my face. I looked up at her.

With tears in her eyes, she nodded. "I promise. No lies."

Seventeen

ESSENCE

IT HAD BEEN a long week and my mind was only on one thing—Shane and I going away for the weekend, courtesy of the points I'd racked up from all my traveling. The only thing I'd told him was to clear his weekend and pack a bag. I thought he would resist just because he'd been so down about everything going on. Since the confrontation, he still hadn't talked to his parents or reached out to Casey. I had brunch with Sahana yesterday just to see if there was anything I should know about how to help him, but she assured me he just had to process it and deal with it in his own time.

I appreciated being able to sit down with her. We had only been texting until that point and, after speaking with her in person, I realized she could use my support as well. She ended up crying and expressing how much this situation was messing with her work and her ability to trust people. I tried to comfort her as best I could, while validating her feelings. She had the right to be upset, just as much as Shane. Her world had been thrown upside down as well.

I finished throwing the last of my toiletries in the bag and closed it up. Myrtle Beach was beautiful around this time of year and I knew we would have a good time. I'd gotten a great bed-and-breakfast right by the beach and was even more excited that it was black-owned. I knew the food would be amazing. My phone lit up as I grabbed the bag and headed toward the living room.

"Hey, Trish. How's that headache?"

"Girl, I swear I'm about to find a crack head to sell me a Percocet. This is crazy."

I laughed. "You better not. It's probably a migraine. Excedrin is the best for those."

"My doctor said my body is changing a lot and this comes with the territory. Hormonal changes."

I grabbed a banana from the kitchen. Shane would be here in a few minutes. Since I was closer to the airport, we were leaving from here.

"I'm so happy you're getting away," she continued. "How's Shane? How are things with you guys?"

I bit into the banana, grateful for the pause. Nobody knew what was going on and I wanted to keep it that way, but it was hard with Trish. She was my sister, for real.

"He's good. Just a lot going on with the season getting ready to start back up. He's just stressed. Figured a little getaway would be perfect for him."

"How are you going to maintain your abstinence around all that fineness up at some fancy bed-and-breakfast?"

I almost spit. "The same way I do here. Separate rooms."

She chuckled. "I have to give it to you, sis. You're holding it down."

I stopped chewing. "Did you slip?"

There was silence. "Almost."

"Listen, it's all good. God knows it's hard out here trying to stay abstinent. On top of that, He sends us both men that look like they stepped off the cover of GQ."

"Exactly, but I'm trying. I didn't come this far to only come this far."

"Why don't I pray over both of us? It's clear we need it."

I said a quick prayer, then we discussed a few business things before hanging up. Just as I ended the call, Shane's name popped up on my phone.

"Perfect timing," I said, answering. "I just hung up with Trish."

"I'm on my way up, Baby Girl."

"Okay."

I noticed Shane still called, although he had a key. I appreciated that he respected my space and wanted me to feel comfortable, but he was the first man I had given a key to. I wanted him to use it. I texted Winter and Remi as I waited for him. Trish and I were going to have a meeting about Remi when I returned. As much as we wanted it to, it just wasn't working out with her.

I turned at the sound of the key in the door. When he opened it and stepped inside, I smiled.

"You used your key," I said, walking over to him. "Finally."

He kissed me. "I don't know why I wasn't using it. Maybe I was overthinking it all."

He placed his bag down. "My Uber driver talked my head off all the way here. I'm a pretty nice guy, but he had me ready to tell him to shut up. All he talked about was basketball."

I pinched his cheeks. "Awww, poor baby. It must suck to have so many fans," I teased.

He grabbed my hand and led me to the couch. "You know what I mean."

"Babe, it was probably his first time having a superstar in his car. That's a big deal for any kid."

He shrugged. "I know. That's why I didn't say anything. Don't tell me you're going to be one of those people that makes me feel bad for being human."

"Of course not."

I looked at his face. I could tell he hadn't been sleeping. Hopefully, he'd rest on the trip.

"I think we need to head out now. I already requested an Uber."

We stood up.

"I didn't have breakfast," he said. "I guess I'll grab something in the airport."

I went into the kitchen, then came back, carrying some fruit. "I had a banana. These will have to do until we get to the airport."

I threw him an apple and a pear. Catching them effortlessly, he bit into the apple, leaving only half on the stem.

"Gross," I teased.

He finished the fruit quickly, then grabbed our bags and we headed downstairs.

"Thanks for this, babe. Much needed," he said, as we sat on the lobby bench.

"Just promise me you'll relax and have a good time."

I grabbed his face, kissing him several times before looking at him.

"I promise. I will."

Eighteen

ESSENCE

WE ENDED up having the best time. Shane really let loose and enjoyed himself. I thought three days wouldn't be enough, but he fooled me. We filled those three days up with swimming, sitting down by the beach, playing volleyball with some people we met, doing a little shopping and, of course, resting. Now, as we were landing back in Philadelphia, I wished I had added another day or two.

I had a lot to deal with at work and, of course, I was concerned about him falling back into a slump. But like his sister said, I had to give him space to process it the way he needed to. After we got off the plane, we headed to the carpool area where the car services picked people up. We would share an Uber, with me being dropped off first, then him. It took an hour before we were finally on our way home. I knew coming back during rush hour wasn't the best idea, but the free flights were always the ones that had the worst times.

"We have to do this again soon," he said, as he looked out into traffic. "My treat next time."

I gave a lopsided grin. "Can't wait. Next time, we have to do at least a week."

He grabbed my hand. "Deal."

We rode the rest of the way home in silence. Once we pulled up to my spot, he helped me with my bag and rode all the way up with me.

"I love you," he said, holding me tight as we hugged. "I'll call you when I get in. Get some rest."

"I love you more."

He kissed my forehead, then left.

I locked the door behind him, then walked right over to the couch and plopped down. Traveling was tiring. Throwing my legs up, I grabbed the fleece blanket that laid across my sofa, threw it on my body and fell asleep.

* * *

I SET my latte down and opened my laptop. Looking around at my office, I realized how three days away felt like a week, especially as I checked all my work emails. I replied to the ones that were urgent, marking the other ones to be answered later. Trish was on her way in. Winter was in the studio downstairs, warming up. We were recording two new songs for her today. I hadn't heard from Remi yet, but Trish told me we needed to talk, so I knew more drama must've ensued while I was away.

This girl was becoming a thorn in my side. All she had to do was make it past her ninety days, and she would be able to officially sign, giving her one of the best distribution deals in the industry. Winter was younger than her and less experienced, yet she was proving to be a more mature artist. I wasn't judgmental, but I wondered if Remi's behavior had anything to do with her getting involved in all these New Age practices. Most people who burned sage, played with crystals and did stuff with chakras didn't realize they were opening a door to the enemy.

Remi was a huge advocate of all of this stuff. Growing up in the church, I knew exactly what to look for when it came to people being used by the enemy. Sometimes, they didn't even realize it. That was the thing with all this new stuff—nobody tells you you're literally inviting the enemy in and playing on his turf. Whatever it was, I was sick of it. She had the voice and she definitely had the looks, but her attitude was off-putting at best.

Standing up, I headed down to the studio. I couldn't help but smile at the plaques and awards that lined the wall as I walked toward the elevator. One of the reasons I had chosen this building when I first got it was because I could have an office on one floor and a studio on the other. It was perfect for business and Trish and I had made millions in this building. The elevator doors chimed, and I stepped on. Resting against the wall of the elevator, I felt the excitement growing as I got to the basement.

My smile quickly faded when the elevator doors opened. The studio was right in front of the elevator, and since everything was glass, anyone could see right into the studio. I could tell by the way Remi's head was moving and by the strained look on Trish's face, I had walked into a fire that would need to be put out.

"What is going on in here?" I asked, barging in. "I could hear you guys before the elevator doors opened."

Remi snatched her head in my direction. "You guys are the most unprofessional managers I've ever worked with. I specifically requested to be put on tour with Kehlani because I knew she was going to say yes. We have a relationship. There's at least four things on my request list that haven't even been discussed yet."

I looked over at Winter, who had stepped out of the booth.

"Guys, I'm ready," she said softly.

I knew she was trying to disrupt so we could stay focused.

"Don't you hear us having a meeting?" Remi said, now looking at her. "Trust me, your little songs will get recorded. Calm down."

Winter's eyes widened. "I wasn't talking to you. I was talking to my managers."

Remi threw her hands on her hips. "Your managers? *Our* managers. And don't think I haven't noticed what's going on here." She looked at all three of us. "I know there's favoritism."

Trish threw her hands up. "First of all, Winter was signed before you. A whole year before you. Second, you haven't even been with us for two full months and you think everything you requested is going to get done," she said.

"And last," I interjected, "you don't tell us how things go. Anything you submitted to us were suggestions, and your probationary contract outlines that. We made it very clear to your attorney as well. You signed it."

I had my arms crossed over my chest, standing like I was confronting a bully. This was it for me. Remi was done. We just had to make it official, but we wouldn't do that in front of Winter. It wasn't professional. I had a business trip coming up and Trish and I had already decided that we would release her once I got back. Today was just confirmation.

"Remi, it doesn't seem like you're happy here and we recognize that," I continued. "For now, you need to leave or go down to the other studio and do some writing. We have to get ready for Winter's session."

I moved around her and sat at the soundboard. Trish followed suit and Winter walked back into the booth. If there was one thing I learned, it was to never give a bully any more energy than you had to. Remi hated being ignored, but she also knew when to back down.

"So, who's working with me? Why does Winter need both of you in here?"

Trish whirled around in her chair. "Until now, you weren't even talking about working. You weren't scheduled to be here. You stormed in here because you don't like when someone else is getting attention. What? Did you see Winter's name down on the recording schedule and you decided to crash?"

I smirked.

"Besides, Dev Hits is expecting both of us to be here."

"Wait... hold up. She's working with Dev? What about me?"

I watched Winter shake her head, then place the headphones on. I wanted to ignore Remi, but I had one more thing to say. I whirled my chair around and looked at her.

"Remi, you may not be used to this, but we're the bosses when it comes to Taylor Made Music Group. Dev, as you call him, requested to work with Winter because he knows she isn't a diva. Let this be the last time you talk to us like you run something here, because you don't pay one bill up in here. Now, dismiss yourself before I say something I'm gonna regret."

I wasn't sure whether it was the tone in my voice or the look I gave her, but her hands slowly dropped to her side. She glared at me for a few seconds, then stormed out, mumbling something under her breath. I turned back to the soundboard and gave Winter the signal.

"Let's run a few practices before Dev gets here," I said.

We all shared a laugh, then Winter started singing. I closed my eyes, grooving to her sultry voice. I was in my element.

* * *

AFTER SEVEN STRAIGHT hours of recording, I was finally leaving the studio. Despite the fiasco from this morning, the day was actually super productive and exciting. It ended on a high note when Dev Hits decided he was going to officially come on to help produce the rest of Winter's album. This helped tremendously because it meant she could have an earlier release. I was on cloud nine as I drove home. Remi had called me twice since I left the studio, but I sent her to voicemail.

I stopped at a red light as my phone rang again. I didn't even look to see who was calling. I sent it straight to voicemail. Shane and I were meeting up in the morning and I would call him once I got home, so anyone else could leave a message. I was jamming to Winter's new song when my phone rang again.

"Remi. Go away, girl. Please, kick rocks," I said out loud.

I finally looked at the Bluetooth screen and saw my father's name flashing across it.

"Why is he blowing me up like this?" I said, grabbing my phone to try to send him a quick text.

Waiting until I arrived at another red light, I looked down at my phone. Just when I was about to send him a text, he was sending me one.

"What is it, Dad?"

I looked at the text. My mouth fell open and my heart started racing. "No. No. No. She wouldn't have..."

A horn blared and I looked up in the rearview mirror. The light had changed. I thanked the driver as I hit the gas. I had to pull over. I saw a CVS to my right and quickly pulled into the parking lot. Putting the car in park, I read the headline again.

Shane Bishop Facing Family Challenges Weeks Before Training Camp

I READ THE ARTICLE. It was out. All of it was out. Somebody had leaked the story to the press. I tried calling him.

"Shane, pick up, baby. Please pick up."

His phone kept going to voicemail. After two more attempts, I threw my phone down and pulled out of the parking lot, doing eighty all the way to his place.

* * *

IT WAS ridiculous how quickly the press got hold of a story. When I pulled up to Shane's, there were several news vans waiting outside. The fact that an athlete's address was available to anyone was maddening enough. I hopped out of my car and rushed up to his door. Speaking of keys, this was the first time I would use the one I had to his place. I whispered a quick thank you to God that I had it with me. I had just put it on my key ring with my car keys right around the time we found everything out.

"Ms. Taylor," a voice behind me said. "Do you care to comment? How is Shane doing? Is it true that his biological father is a dead man? How are you helping him get through this?"

I made it inside just as the cameras started flashing. I locked the door and turned, racing through the rooms to find him. Finally, I found him in his home office on the third floor. When he looked at me, he shook his head.

"She told them," he said.

His voice was low.

"How could she do this to me?"

I walked over to him, grabbing him in a hug. "Baby, I'm so sorry. Casey promised this wasn't about money or anything other than finding you. Why would she do this?"

He handed me his phone. It was going off like crazy.

"She told me she didn't do it. I called her. She said she kept her word. She doesn't know how it got out."

I looked down at his phone, lighting up. Finally, I stopped it, turning it on silent.

"Baby, do you think she told somebody else?"

He cut his eyes at me. "It was her. The article said, "The sister of Shane Bishop says..." I know they aren't talking about Sahana."

I nodded. He was right. The article mentioned only his sister. It was Casey. At this point, I didn't care about that. This was bad. Shane's mental state was already pretty fragile before the story leaked. Now, I was afraid he would really break. He looked out the window of his office. I could hear the reporters's voices down below. Slowly, he turned around. His eyes widened as he quickly walked over to me.

"What, babe? What's wrong?"

"My parents."

He immediately went into action. He grabbed his phone and made a phone call.

"Bring them here. And Sahana, too. I don't know and I don't care how you do it. Bring them here. I'll get rid of the reporters."

He made a few more requests, then hung up.

"No matter what, they're still my parents. I don't want the paparazzi bothering them at home."

"Babe, you're right. Family is family."

He looked at me. "What is God trying to teach me with all this?"

I didn't have the answers. At all. Whatever God was doing, I hoped it would start making sense to us soon.

"Babe, let's pray."

"No!"

I jumped. He walked closer to me, grabbing me in a hug.

"I'm sorry. I didn't mean to yell. It's just... I don't want to pray right now."

"Then we won't. What do you want to do?"

He pulled back from our hug, then looked at his desk. "Nothing. I just want my parents and sister here with me and I don't want to do nothing. I can't fix this."

He was right. It would take a miracle from God to turn this whole thing around. But he had the right idea. Bringing his family here would present a united front. As he sat back down in his chair, I prayed under my breath. He may not have wanted to pray, but it didn't mean prayer wasn't needed.

Nineteen

SHANE

I KNEW I was drinking too much, but it was my homeboy Kevell's birthday party, and I was letting loose. I'd had way too many Long Island Iced Teas and I could tell from the way I was wobbling, I needed to slow down. I collapsed on the lounge chair by the pool, pushing aside someone's towel as I threw my legs up. I pulled my phone out and checked to see if Essence had reached out. I hated she was out of town, but she'd been there for me like crazy over the last few weeks.

With only two weeks before training camp, I was trying to stay as focused as possible. I couldn't believe Casey had betrayed my trust. I should've made her sign an NDA like she'd been saying, but I guess it was all a front for her to destroy me. I opened the browser on my phone and re-read the article for the thousandth time.

Basketball sensation Shane Bishop is having trouble during the off season, but it's not the kind of trouble you'd expect. Sources close to the family say that the man that's been raising him is not his biological father. Apparently, this news comes from a sister that Shane knew nothing about, and sources confirm that there is DNA evidence.

I closed the browser and threw my phone on the chair. I looked up to see a few women waving at me in the pool. They were waving me over. Smiling, I leaned up and started taking my shirt off.

"Don't even think about it."

I closed my eyes, despising the sound of my sister's voice at this moment.

"I don't even know why I brought you with me," I said.

"Because you and I both know you need someone to keep an eye on you," she said, throwing her legs up on the chair next to mine. "Don't do something stupid because you're upset with our parents. Essence doesn't deserve that," she finished, eyeing the girls with a scowl on her face. "Shame on them heifers for even trying to take advantage. They've read the news."

She looked at me. I stared straight ahead, trying my best not to break. The drinking was merely a coverup, but if I wasn't here, I'd be home, curled up in a ball, praying away the darkness.

"Bro, I know things are crazy right now—"

"Don't do that."

She placed her hand on my arm. "Dad feels really bad."

I snapped my head in her direction. I leaned closer to her so nobody could hear me. "I bet he does. He's a liar!"

"He was protecting his wife and our family."

I smirked. "He was making sure he didn't get busted. Listen, you're his child, so you have no idea how I feel. Don't make excuses for them."

The sadness in her eyes made me grab her hand. "Sis, I'm sorry. I don't mean to be so cold, but you have to let me deal with this in my way."

She looked at the empty glass on the ground next to me. "Not if it means drowning your sorrows out with drinking and flirting with other women."

I laid back against the chair and closed my eyes. "You know this is how I am. I spend a few weeks wallowing in sorrow, then I get myself together and push through. Don't judge."

She hit my leg. "I'm not. I'm concerned. All I'm saying is, don't let the enemy win. He wants to see you spiral out of control because of all this."

I took a few deep breaths, then responded. "I don't understand why Casey would betray me. Now, I'll never reach out to her."

"I've been asking myself the same thing, but I've been wondering, what if it was someone else?"

I sat up. "She was the only one there other than Essence."

She raised an eyebrow. "But she said her mother didn't want her to reach out. Could it have been her?"

I thought about it. To be honest, I'd been so focused on Casey, I hadn't even thought about her mother.

"And," Sahana continued, "who's to say her mother didn't tell others? You don't know, Shane. This honestly may have more legs than you think."

I sat in silence, contemplating everything she said. We all had accused Casey on the spot. It was what made sense at the time.

"Where is all this coming from? You were so sure when the article first dropped," I asked.

Sighing, she leaned in closer to me. "Let's just say I've always had my doubts. I wasn't there when you sat with Casey, but I've been doing my homework. Her mother did a stint in rehab when Casey was eight. She actually didn't have her daughter for a whole year. Maybe she relapsed because of all this?"

I listened intently. "When were you going to tell me you'd been playing Nancy Drew and had new information?"

"I was going to wait, but seeing you like this hurts my heart, big bro," she said softly. "I don't want to lose another brother."

My words caught in my throat. Sahana only brought up our brother Samuel when she was really afraid. I looked at her and grabbed both of her hands.

"You won't. I promise."

Looking around, I saw Kevell and my other teammates waving me over to the DJ booth. One of the party girls he had hired was carrying a large cake. I knew they were about to sing happy birthday to Kevell. I stood up, fixing my shirt and grabbing the empty glass. Sahana stood up. I leaned in and hugged her. I absorbed my sister's hug, leaning into it as if it were our last.

"Thanks for the chat. Keep me posted on what you find out. I just want whoever said something to pay."

We headed over toward Kevell and the crew. "To be honest, bro, there's nothing you can really do. There's no law against revealing somebody's secret, especially if an NDA wasn't involved. To be fair, whether it was Casey or her mother, it's their secret, too."

I scoffed, not wanting to hear that. Somebody was going to pay, even if God was the one that had to handle the situation.

* * *

THIS WAS the fourth time I'd gone to the bathroom in the last hour. I regretted all the drinks I'd had. After flushing, I stood in front of the bathroom mirror, laughing at how elaborate Kevell's bathroom was. You would think he was married with all the toiletries he had set up in such a fancy way. Chuckling, I washed my hands, then threw some water on my face. Drying off with a hand towel, I balanced myself before turning to head out. Before I could open the door, it was pushed open.

"Hey, somebody's in here. It was closed for a reason," I snapped.

It was my fault I'd forgotten to lock it. Everyone was downstairs, partying, and Kevell had six bathrooms in his house. I didn't even think it was an issue.

"I know. That's why I'm coming in," a female voice said.

When she stepped into full view, I frowned. "Remi? What are you doing in here?"

She walked closer to me, her breasts hanging out of her bikini top. As she sashayed over to me, I realized what was happening. I tried stepping around her, but she blocked me.

"Oh, what's wrong? You can't have a little fun while Wifey is out of town?" She placed her finger on my lip. "Shhhh. Nobody has to know."

I looked toward the door, happy she'd left it cracked. I guess she thought she closed it.

"Look, I don't know what's going on, but I don't even get down like that. You know I love Essence more than anything, and even if I was single, I wouldn't touch you."

Her smile faded.

"Please. Half your basketball team is constantly in my DMs. Don't play yourself," she said, placing her hand on my chest.

"Move."

THE ESSENCE OF HIS SOUL

I stepped around her, trying my hardest not to touch her. If I moved her, I would be in trouble for assault. If I didn't, I could get in trouble for a lot worse.

I backed up a few steps, just to put space between us.

"You're foul. Essence is your manager and she's been pushing your career like crazy," I continued, searching my pockets for my phone. Shoot. I left it on the lounge chair. I hadn't even noticed. Now, I had no way to record for proof.

God, help me out of this. Please.

Finally, I decided I'd rather be accused of assault than rape. I felt like she was trying to set me up.

"I'm going to tell you one last time. Move."

This time, when she tried to stop me, I pushed hard.

"Hey!" she shouted, falling back against the ceramic tile wall that was wrapped around the shower.

When I heard the noise, I knew she'd hit her back, but I was grateful she hadn't hit her head. I pulled the door open all the way and left without turning back. Shaking my head, I headed to the pool to grab my phone. I knew I couldn't keep this from Essence. If I did, Remi would try to spin this in her favor. I prayed Remi would just let this go and move on. For some reason, I knew rejection wasn't something she was used to. Because of that, I had to watch my back.

***

MY PHONE RANG, but my head was pounding. I rolled over and threw a pillow over my head, trying to block out the noise. I was never drinking like that again. The ringing finally stopped. I threw the pillow off me, then slowly got up. I felt like I had a gallon of water in my bladder that needed to come out. I trudged to the bathroom, still half asleep. After I came out, my phone started ringing again.

"What?" I said, without looking at the phone. I didn't even bother with my AirPods.

"Well, good morning to you, too, handsome."

At the sound of Essence's voice, I jolted fully awake. "Baby, hey. What's going on?"

"You sound like you had too much of a good time last night," she said. "I just wanted to call you before I head into my next meeting. I tried calling last night to be sure you made it home safe. I called Sahana when I didn't get you. You good?"

I dropped my head in my other hand. I didn't call her and tell her what happened yet because I was still trying to figure out how to tell her that her artist came on to me without messing up her money. I knew Essence would want to fire her.

"I'm okay, baby. Just... tired. A lot going on."

I heard her moving around in the background.

"What's wrong, baby? Something else happen?"

My mouth was extremely dry. "Sahana found out some details about Casey's mother. She's not so sure it was Casey that leaked the secret."

"Yes, thank you so much," I heard her say. "Sorry, baby. I was finishing up my breakfast at the hotel restaurant. So, Sahana's been playing lawyer, I see. I love it. She's your sister and she's supposed to have your back."

I stood up. "I know, I know. I'll fill you in when you get back. I never thought a three-day trip felt so long. I miss you."

"I miss you more, baby. One more day, then I'll be home. I really hated leaving you with everything going on."

"Nonsense. You've been my rock this entire time." I looked at the clock on my bedstand. It was almost eleven in the morning. I needed to get my day started. "I'll meet you at the airport tomorrow. Call me when you land."

"Of course. But we'll talk tonight."

"Yes. Tonight. I love you."

I knew I was rushing her off the phone, but I needed to handle this the right way.

"Love you, babe."

I hung up with a quick bye. Why was I acting so nervous? Remi was the one who was wrong. I was innocent.

"Shane, just get in the shower, pray, and ask God for direction. He's not going to leave you now."

I headed back into the bathroom, connecting my Bluetooth speaker and turning on some worship music. I may have acted like a heathen last night, but sobering up made me go right back to my roots. It was always going to be Christ for me. I didn't want to fall down a slippery slope, getting comfortable numbing my pain with things that could turn into addictions. As I brushed my teeth, I realized how asking my sister to go to the party with me had saved me from making other mistakes that could've cost me my relationship. I stopped brushing and decided to pray.

"God, You know this isn't how I like to do things. Part of me being super emotional is that I have really high highs, and really low lows. Help me to always go to You when I'm low. I need Your wisdom for this situation. I pray You step in and show me what to do so I can honor You and my relationship. This thing with my family, I need You to work that out, too. Right now, I feel like I can't trust anyone but You. Help me, God. Amen."

I wiped the tears away and finished brushing my teeth. I hopped in the shower and stayed in for a long time. The steam from the shower felt so good and I needed the relief it brought. Once I stepped out, I grabbed my phone and headed back into my room. I got an Instagram notification. When I opened it, I laughed at the pictures Kevell had posted from the party. The photographer got some dope shots. I was about to close out the app when I saw the message. Opening it, my mouth fell open as I read it.

"Do you see what you did? I'm going to the police and telling them you tried to rape me. This bruise on my back supports my story. If my lawyers and I don't hear from you in twenty-four hours, I'm going to the blogs."

I scrolled through the photos she'd sent. I didn't know if I was concerned with the photos or more concerned that she'd told someone. It was clear these pictures were taken by someone else since most of them were of her back.

"God, I've never given You a deadline, but I need You to come through now before I turn back to my old ways."

Twenty

ESSENCE

36 Hours Later

I COULD TELL by the look on Shane's face that he'd been eating stress for breakfast, lunch, and dinner. I'd been checking in with Sahana and he still hadn't talked to his parents. Until he talked to them, he would continue to create scenarios in his head and listen to the enemy's taunting.

"Hey, babe," I said, hugging him close. "I missed you so much."

He held me tightly around the waist. "I missed you, baby."

I saw his driver loading my bags in the SUV as we finally pulled away.

"I hate asking this, but how's your heart?"

He looked at me. The bags under his eyes spoke first.

"Baby, I just want all of this to be over," he said. "Let's get in. I have to tell you something."

Confusion settling over my heart, I followed his lead as he helped me get into the SUV. I didn't want to bum rush him with questions, but the way he said it, had my stomach fluttering. We put our seatbelts on, and the driver took off. He held my hand but hadn't spoken yet.

God, please don't let this be anything that will make me angry.

"At Kevell's party, something happened."

I eyed him carefully. "What happened?"

He opened his mouth to speak, but before we could say anything, both of our phones started going off. Even the driver's notifications chimed.

"Sorry about that. I meant to put mine on silent," the driver said, looking at us through the rearview mirror.

I tried to ignore mine and keep Shane focused, but it was hard with how many times our phones kept chiming. Then mine rang. Finally, I looked.

"What is going on?" I asked.

"No, no..."

Then I heard him curse. Shane had never cursed before.

I opened the first article link I'd been sent. I read through it, shaking my head as I read. My vision was blurry from the tears that clouded my pupils.

"Shane... what did you do?"

He looked at me, throwing his phone down. "Nothing. I promise you, I didn't do anything."

I looked back down at my phone. "So, these bruises are from what?"

I opened another notification, and there was a link to another article from another outlet. Then another. All of them said the same thing.

SHANE BISHOP IS BEING ACCUSED *of sexual assault by rising R&B superstar, Remi Barrington. This is messy. Now, Remi is signed to Taylor Made Music Group, the label owned by Shane's girlfriend, Essence Taylor.*

OF COURSE, each article worded it differently, but the story was the same. I looked at Shane, unable to speak.

"I was trying to tell you—"

I slapped his arm. "Yeah, now! You should've told me when I called you yesterday morning. That's why you were rushing me off the phone? You thought I didn't notice."

He shook his head. "Baby, let me explain."

I looked around, realizing I had no choice. We were stuck in midday lunch traffic and I couldn't go anywhere.

"You better tell me everything."

Before he could speak, my phone rang again. It was Trish.

"Trish, I can't talk right now," I said. "I know. I saw. I'm with him now. I need to get the details and I'll call you back. I know, I know. Give me an hour. Please. I just landed."

I hung up. "This better be good because I have four artists wanting to know what's going on. I have to explain to my business partner how we might lose our entire roster because of you."

The driver raised the partition, giving us some privacy.

"She came onto me and I pushed her off. That's how she got the bruises," he started.

I listened intently as he told me the story from top to bottom. He even told me how he tried recording it to protect himself, but he didn't have his phone. I sat in silence for a few minutes before responding.

"Shane, I really wish you would've told me and forwarded me her DM so I could've had Trish get ahead of this," I said softly.

I was angry, but not at him. Remi had been a problem since the second week she'd been with us, and while I didn't know of any incidents like this, her diva ways told me she was probably lying. I wasn't saying this just because Shane was my man. I had a lot to lose. I really felt in my heart Shane wouldn't do this, especially with all he was going through. He was already in the media enough lately.

"Baby, this is bad," I continued, checking my phone again. His was still going off.

"I have to call my lawyer. Now."

He called his lawyer, explaining the same thing he explained to me. While he handled his call, I called Trish back. I had expected to put out some fires when I got back, but not fires like this. After twenty minutes of back and forth, my call ended. Trish was going to speak with our lawyers and publicist. I had to meet her at the office right away.

"I have to head to the office. Can you tell the driver there's a change of plans, please?" I said, ignoring a fifth call from my mother.

"Baby, I'm sorry. I thought it was better to tell you face to face. I knew you were coming home."

I wanted to be pissed, but he was right. It wasn't like he had kept it from me for days or weeks. I know I should extend him grace, but for some reason, I wanted him to pay in some way.

"You don't even drink that much. You know your limit. Why did you have to get drunk?" I said, tears filling my eyes again.

He looked at me, then pulled me into him. "You can fuss at me. I'm okay with that. I know this is a mess and I'm so, so sorry. But baby, we need each other."

I sobbed in his arms, thinking about all the damage control Trish and I would have to do. I ignored the rest of my notifications. I needed this time to think and deal with my own emotions. Shane answered his ringing phone.

"Yes, Coach, I know. But I didn't do it. I know, but... wait. What do you mean, suspended? Coach, come on. I've never been in trouble and I would never do something like this," he said. His voice cracked. "Coach, please. But if I don't go to training camp, I can't play."

He threw his phone against the driver's seat.

"I can't believe this."

He slammed his hand against the window. "They don't even care if a man is innocent. The accusation is enough."

A part of me didn't want to, but I grabbed his hand. I had mixed emotions, but I had a decision to make. Either I was going to stand beside him, or I wasn't.

"Look at me," I said forcefully. He turned to face me. "I got you. I believe you. We don't have time to be sad. The enemy is working overtime right now, and we need to be focused. Got it?"

I felt it in my spirit that Shane wasn't lying, and I was going to stick beside him.

"Babe, you don't know how much I needed to hear that."

He leaned over and grabbed me in a hug.

"God, if You brought us to it, You'll bring us through it," I said as we continued the drive to my studio.

It wasn't always easy to pray when faced with hard times, but God was the only person I knew that could turn this thing around without either of us getting burned in the fire.

* * *

"SIS, I don't know if this is good enough," Trish said after re-reading our publicist's statement for the label for the third time. "You think she needs to have Shane's statement in here as well?"

I looked at it, trying to focus on what we were doing. All I could think about was Shane and how he must be feeling. While we could lose all of our artists and it may take a minute to re-sign new people, he could lose everything. His career. Every endorsement. Everything.

"I think it will have to do," I said.

Trish looked at me. She pushed the laptop back, then grabbed me in a hug.

"Listen, I trust you," she said. "I know it looks like the world is against us right now, but I'm not leaving your side."

I hugged her back, fighting back tears. "I was so afraid you'd want to part ways when you heard."

She frowned, pulling away from me. "Girl, we've been sisters for six years now. There's no way I would just believe something like this, especially since we've been having issues with Remi. I just hate that we already drafted her release, and it will look like she's being released because Shane is your man."

"What did Pete say about that? Is there a way to still release her, or will it look bad?"

She pulled up an email on her phone. "Since we have the date that the release was drafted as a week ago, he says it may not look bad, but he thinks we should hold off. She's still in her ninety-day probation we give all clients, so she'll probably release herself with everything going on."

I nodded. "Yeah. Her attorney will probably advise her to part ways because of the conflict of interest."

"Exactly."

I grabbed my phone and ignored another call from my mom. I shot her a text. *Mom, please let me sort through this. I need to focus on my business and figure some things out before I can discuss this.*

I just wanted you to know that I have your back and I love you. I don't believe that girl for one minute. Shane loves you.

Smiling, I texted back a bunch of hearts. I wasn't expecting her to say that. I realized that the last few months had been a huge blessing for our relationship. She'd gone back to the woman who was more concerned about my heart than appearances. My father, who had called me twelve times already, was still being Bishop Taylor. I had six texts from him, saying how I needed to leave Shane alone immediately.

Placing my phone back down, I turned my attention back to Trish.

"What did Winter say?"

She stood up. "I was very pleased to hear Winter say she would push her album back while we worked through this, but her and Remi have had several arguments and I think that's working in our favor. She's more concerned about you, but Coffee Tan is out for sure."

I shook my head, but I saw that coming. He'd been threatening to sign with another label and management company because he wanted the international push we didn't have yet.

"Well, he's been with us for two years. We can part ways amicably."

Trish sucked her teeth. "He was just looking for a reason."

"I know."

My phone lit up. "It's Shane. Give me a minute."

She forced a smile. "Tell him I'm praying for him."

I headed to my private office and closed the door. "Hey, baby. How you holding up?"

"I'm not."

His voice sounded far away.

"What do you need?" I asked.

"Honestly, a vacation. But I can't even leave town."

I sat on the love seat. "Wait. They issued a warrant for your arrest already?"

"I'm turning myself in tomorrow morning. My attorney's advice."

I sighed. "Babe, I'm so sorry, but I see why he said it. Tell your side."

"Essence, I'm a black basketball player with endorsements worth over ten million dollars and a contract worth twice that. I'm already guilty."

I hated he was being negative, but I couldn't imagine being in his shoes.

"Trish says she's praying for you. I think there are more people who believe you than you think."

He cleared his throat. "I don't need people who believe me. I need Remi to tell the truth."

In that moment, all I knew to do was pray. I covered him, crying while praying. When I was done, he was crying, too.

"You comin' by tonight?" he asked.

"You think it would be better for you to come to me? I'm sure you'll have reporters outside your house. At least with my condo, they can't come upstairs."

"Yeah. That's why I'm at my parents. I didn't want to go home."

I stayed silent. *He's at his parents? I hope they talked.*

"How's being there with all this going on?"

"I'll tell you tonight," he said. "I gotta go. My lawyer is clicking in. Love you."

"Love you more. Babe, we'll get through this."

"I hope so."

I ended the call and leaned back against the love seat. I said it to him, but I was encouraging myself as well. They were already calling me all types of names on social media because I hadn't spoken out on behalf of Remi yet. In this post-Me Too era, if you weren't on the woman's side automatically, you were complicit with the alleged rapist. I hated this. Everyone had a right to a fair trial and not all women were innocent in these situations.

I was going to post my statement tonight, but I had to wait until the publicist worked on what I sent her. I wanted to show I wasn't going to be bullied into taking her side, but I wanted to show I was supportive of women as well. There was a way to kill two birds with one stone—supporting my man and supporting women who were truly victims in these situations. Trish knocked on the glass. I stood up and opened the door.

"Our individual statements are ready."

We walked back over to the desk and grabbed our laptops.

"Girl, I hope we get to see why we pay her the big bucks. This is a time where she needs to bring her A game," Trish said.

"Who you tellin'?"

I opened my email and read the statement. As I reached the bottom, all I could do was thank God we hired a publicist who had a way with words, just like we did. I was thoroughly pleased.

Essence's Statement

Being a woman in this business is never easy and I stand beside any woman who experiences the pain that comes from incidents like this. However, I do believe there are two victims in this situation. I step outside of being a girlfriend and I've put myself in Remi's shoes. What saddens me is that Remi didn't feel like she could come to me as her manager, or even my partner, Trish. We would've listened and protected her. Instead, she chose to run to the blogs before even calling her attorney, which there is evidence of. I am in no way victim blaming or shaming, but I'm stating facts based on evidence. She gave Shane twenty-four hours to respond to her before she would run to the blogs. This doesn't sound like a woman who was hurt that she had been assaulted, but like a woman who was pissed she didn't get her way. I won't be bullied into taking a woman's side automatically, but I will say that Shane and I are both praying for the truth to come out and that God will redeem this situation so that everyone can walk away unscathed. In the meantime, we ask that you all don't rush to judgment or cancel culture but allow the events to play out as they need to in order for the truth to be realized. Sincerely, Essence Taylor

Twenty-One

SHANE

I LOOKED over at my parents as I continued making breakfast for all of us. They'd been staying with me the last couple of days and supporting me in ways I really needed. The last week had been draining and emotional. The one good thing that came out of all the drama was that it forced us to talk. We discussed everything and my parents allowed me to ask all the questions I needed. We weren't all the way good, but we were better than we had been a couple of weeks ago. Sahana walked into the kitchen, wiping the sleep from her eyes as she sauntered in.

"Can you put chocolate chips in my pancakes?" she asked.

Smiling, I grabbed the chocolate chips that were hiding behind the pancake box.

"Already ahead of you."

"Thanks, big bro."

My mother stood up and grabbed the oranges to make the fresh squeezed orange juice, while my father sat and read his Bible at the kitchen counter. The silence was killing me, but I knew we all had a bunch of thoughts running through our heads. Finally, Sahana spoke.

"I can't believe how Remi is still on social media, living her best life like nothing is going on," she said.

I poured another pancake, then looked at her. "Why are you following her?"

"I'm not, but she's everywhere. They're posting her social media posts on regular news outlets. Trust me. I have no reason to follow her."

I turned back to the stove. This situation was wearing me out, but I had to give it all my attention. I no longer had time to worry about my personal situation; the professional one took precedence right now. Unless all of this was resolved within the next week, I wouldn't be able to attend training camp and I was suspended until further notice. My phone lit up. I smiled when I saw her name.

"Hey, everyone. Essence just pulled up."

Sahana jumped up and headed to the door. They'd become closer over the last few weeks, which was another bright side to this. It seemed like the storms in my life were creating bonds.

"Hey, family," she said, hugging my mom and dad. "How's everyone feeling?"

My dad shrugged. "Trying to hold on," he replied, his voice hoarse.

I'd been paying careful attention to him. His voice had been sounding that way for the last few days. I chalked it up to him probably not sleeping much, but with his heart issues, I was keeping an eye on him.

"How are you, is the question?" my mom asked. "You've been such a big support to our baby boy during this time. I know it hasn't been easy with how people are attacking you, too."

She walked over to me and hugged me around the waist. "I'm trying," she said. "Coffee wanted to leave, so this just gave him a reason and Remi, well…"

I kept staring at the pancakes. Essence had already confided in me that Remi was an issue for the company and the situation with me had made it easier for her to part ways.

"At least she left on her own," Sahana said. "I just hate she's making it look like she left because you didn't have her back."

Essence sighed. "Well, one thing that has worked in our favor is her track record with other managers and the evidence we have of the problems she was causing. I don't have to prove anything to anyone, but it's good to know we have it."

She looked over at me. "Babe, it's all good. Things will work out. People know Remi is a drama queen that likes attention."

I nodded. "You want chocolate chips in your pancakes, too?" I asked her.

"Uh, no. Who's eating chocolate chips in their pancakes?"

Everyone laughed as we pointed at Sahana. Essence finished helping me cook and then, we all sat down to eat. I had to admit, I was absorbing these moments of normalcy. In the last two weeks, I'd gotten at least two hundred emails, six hundred social media notifications and a bunch of personal phone calls I just couldn't handle. Not to mention, the social media comments that had people calling me everything from a bastard child to a rapist. I tried to stay off social, but it was hard. Sometimes I went on there just to see what the supporters were saying. I needed all the encouragement I could get.

"Well, all of this is looking good. Nothing like a man who can cook," Essence said, helping me set out the food that was already done.

"Don't I know it," my mom said.

I forced a smile. My father had always been a great cook, which was one of the things I appreciated about him. He never put it all on my mother to do the domestic stuff. He helped out.

"Look at that bacon," Sahana said, grabbing a piece as Essence placed it on the counter.

"Mom, tell her to stop," I teased. "Did you even wash your hands?"

She stuck her tongue out at me.

After another ten minutes, everything was ready. I joined my family at the counter, and as my dad blessed the food, I snuck a look at Essence. There was something about her presence that just made all of this better. As we ate, we made conversation about everything from the weather to the violence in Philly. I could tell everyone was trying to avoid talking about sports or the upcoming season.

"Essence, I've been wondering, have you ever thought about writing a book?" Sahana asked.

She took a sip of her orange juice, then looked up at the ceiling. "I never really thought about it. Why do you ask?"

Sahana shrugged. "I don't know. I just think being a black woman in music is challenging and people want to know how to do it. Not to mention the PK angle. How do you pursue a career your family hates?"

"Now, that's certainly an interesting angle, but with all the drama that comes with the business, I wouldn't want to add to that. Writing a book about my life as a PK would require me to write about my father. Definitely not a good idea."

I thought about what she said. Maybe it wasn't a good idea, but it had me thinking.

"What if we wrote one together?"

She shifted her attention to me. "What?"

"I mean, once all of this blows over, there will certainly be a story left behind. Even if we don't write about this, we could certainly encourage young people who look like us to pursue what God places in their hearts over what their parents want them to do."

My father cleared his throat. "I think we gave you a choice. Don't you, Shandra?"

I dropped my fork. "Well, it depends on what you mean by choice. You guys encouraged us to go after our dreams, but you definitely emphasized the things you wanted us to do more."

Sahana glanced at our father. Silence fell over the room for a few minutes.

"I think all parents just want their children to have successful careers," my mother said.

"Yeah, but it shouldn't have to be such a fight."

My father looked at Sahana. "Do you feel we forced you to go to law school?"

She didn't say anything. I looked at her, hoping she would finally share what she'd been telling me for the last four years. Finally, she spoke.

"Well, I wanted to take a year off to figure things out, but you guys made it seem like it wasn't an option. I think Shane is just pointing out the obvious—it's hard being a preacher's kid."

"Oh, like you guys had it so bad," my mother said. "Listen, I know there's a lot going on right now and you're probably frustrated, but Shane, we gave you guys a wonderful childhood. You didn't have to ask for anything."

I pushed my plate away from me. "Well, it seems like my childhood would've been a lot different had my real father been alive."

When I heard Essence's fork drop, I knew I had gone too far.

"Babe, come on," she said, reaching for my hand. "Let's not do this now."

I pushed away from the counter and stood up. "Why not? Everything's a big mess, anyway. Why not just get it all out in the open so we can all just move on?"

I looked at everyone before I walked out of the kitchen and headed to my bedroom. I closed the door behind me, hoping nobody would follow. Right now, even seeing Essence would frustrate me a little. I needed to be alone. I walked toward my bed, but before I could reach it, I dropped to my knees, sobbing in my hands the whole way down.

* * *

I TAPPED my feet on the carpet, grateful the floor wasn't hardwood. Otherwise, I would probably end up agitating the other people waiting to see their therapist. Since everything had happened, I'd been to therapy once a week, but after my explosion yesterday, I still felt off. I knew I couldn't rush the process, but I hated how I was snapping on everyone. Even if my parents deserved it, I didn't like not being in control of my emotions. Crying was one thing, but anger was different.

"Hey, aren't you that basketball player?" a female voice said, breaking me out of my thoughts.

I looked up at her without responding.

"You got a lot going on. I guess you do need to talk to someone."

I forced a smile. I wasn't sure if she was about to curse me out or throw something at me, so I remained silent.

"Did you do it?" she continued. "Assault that girl?"

I stared at her for a few seconds, then shrugged. "Would you believe me?"

She cocked her head to the side. The other patrons who had been waiting were now staring at me. It was as if everyone wanted to hear the answer.

"Well, did you?"

I took a deep breath. "No. I didn't. I swear I didn't."

My publicist and attorney had been issuing statements since all of this blew up, but how often did someone actually get to ask a celebrity about the accusations circulating around?

"If you didn't, then she'll pay for lying. But if you did, you might just have to leave the city altogether."

"Kelly, Dr. Ramone is ready," the receptionist said.

The girl who had been talking to me stood up, gave me a long look, then walked away. I wasn't sure what to say.

"Pssst... pssst..."

I turned my head in the direction of the noise.

"These women be lying. I don't think you did it. I know you'll beat this."

More silence. While it felt good for someone to have my back, something about him saying, "these women be lying", felt eerie.

God, please just let this all be over soon. Please.

"Thanks," was all I said as the receptionist called my name next. I rushed toward my therapist's office.

Once inside, I dropped on the couch. "Doc, I may need a double session. How much time you got for me today?"

Twenty-Two

ESSENCE

WHEN MY DOORMAN told me my father was downstairs, I almost didn't let him up. He was already annoyed with the personal family drama Shane was dealing with, but the sexual assault allegation had him blowing me up, demanding for me to break up with Shane before it ruined my career, a career he never cared about. I knew it was all just manipulation, but since I would have to see him at some point, I let him up.

There was a time I thought I was running from the issues between my dad and I. I used to answer the phone all the time and go back and forth with him about every little thing. It was around my early twenties that I realized it was pointless. That was around the time I finally decided not to take the youth pastor position at my parents' church. My father actually thought he was doing me a favor by allowing me to take the position, although I had dropped out of seminary.

But once I decided on a career in music, completely declining any opportunity that was tied to his or anyone else's ministry, the shift happened. It became more difficult to have a conversation with him and he became more stubborn as the years passed. It was his way, or the highway. It was hard for a man like my father to accept that he couldn't control my life. Sadly, I think my mother had some dreams she wanted to pursue, but being first lady was her priority. It made him happy.

"It's about time you let me up," he said as soon as I opened the door.

I moved to the side so he could enter, ignoring his comment.

"How are you, Dad?"

I followed him to the couch.

"That's all you have to say after ignoring my calls for the last few weeks. I've had to hear how you're doing through your mother."

"I texted. I told you I was fine."

He grunted. "I'm your father. You answer my call."

I sat back against the couch, eyeing him carefully. There was a part of me that wanted to go toe to toe with this man and get it over with, but the other part of me, the part Shane was having an effect on, was willing to humble myself and try to understand my dad's own trauma. His father had, too, been a pastor, and my father had no choice but to go into ministry.

"Dad, what is this really about? You know I'm not breaking up with Shane and I'm definitely not dating someone you picked for me." I crossed my arms. "Can we just talk about what's really bothering you so we can stop revisiting this same old argument?"

"I don't know what you're talking about," he said. "All of this drama with this boy is tarnishing your image."

I raised an eyebrow. "You mean, tarnishing your family's last name, right?"

He winced. "Watch your mouth."

I closed my eyes and prayed in my mind. I needed to prepare myself to say what he'd been avoiding all of my life.

"Dad, can we just say it? You're upset that I'm not the boy you prayed for. You got a little girl when you wanted a boy that you could pass your legacy down to."

When I saw his jaw clench, I knew I had hit a soft spot.

"I can't help that God got in the way of your plans."

"Essence, this is why I didn't want you in that dark industry. Look at how you're talking," he responded, throwing his hands around. "Nothing but the devil."

I chuckled. "I'm sure you would know."

He stood up over me. "Now, you're trying me."

I was raised never to disrespect my parents, and as I watched him standing over me with his nostrils flaring, I realized I had gone too far.

"Listen, I apologize. I know I shouldn't talk to you like that, but can you blame me? You've been being so difficult and treating me crazy ever since I dropped out of seminary. I'm not your puppet."

He slowly sat back down. "I never said you were. I had a life planned out for you and you just threw it away, for what? An unstable career in one of the darkest industries known to man? Honey, you see what's going on. Your artists are leaving, and all of this will probably make it harder to sign new people. It's a sign from God."

I shook my head. There was no point. My father would never see things my way. He would always have it in his mind that I chose the wrong path.

"I'm not leaving Shane, and I'm not leaving music," I said, getting up to head to the kitchen. "Did you want me to make you a plate?"

I heard him moving around in the living room. I was pissed at myself because of the tears that now stung my eyes. I refused to let them fall while he was here. I'd spent enough time in therapy and prayer, working through my daddy issues. I wasn't going to keep letting him hurt me.

"Your mother needs me back home," he said, his voice drifting into the kitchen.

I wiped at my eyes, then headed back into the living room. "Tell her I'll call her later."

I stood in front of him and looked up at him. For a minute, I was that ten-year-old little girl again who saw nothing but a hero when she looked at her father, but it only lasted a minute when he kissed my forehead quickly, then headed to my front door.

"When all of this blows up in your face, don't call me, begging for a job at the church. I love you, but I won't let you bring all of this to my front door."

I jumped when the door slammed. I dropped to my knees. I didn't want to, but I couldn't stop the tears that fell.

THE ESSENCE OF HIS SOUL

* * *

I WAS SO glad we decided to order in and just relax. Shane stroked my arm as I laid across his lap. I called him a few hours after my dad left and he rushed right over. I was learning not to see my problems as an issue for him just because he was going through a lot, but to see them as a way for him to escape his own.

"I'm sorry he's still not willing to hear your heart," Shane said.

Groaning, I turned over to face him. "It's weird because I've actually been thinking about something he said."

He squinted as he stared at me. "Wait. You feel like there's actually something your father said that made sense?"

I leaned up. My phone went off just as I was about to respond. I checked my Instagram notifications.

How can you stay with a rapist? Don't come crying to social media when it happens to you.

You really believe him? He's a basketball player. This isn't surprising.

Women like you make us look bad.

When I saw the negative string of comments on my last picture, I closed the Instagram app immediately. I hadn't posted since all of this came out, but people were still leaving comments on my social media.

"What's wrong?"

I threw the phone down and sighed. "The hate comments. They are getting worse and worse."

He grabbed my hand. "I'm sorry, babe. I hate that you're being targeted because of my mess."

"It sucks how fast this spiraled. Remi knew just what she was doing."

I looked down at my phone again. He grabbed it off the couch and placed it face down on the coffee table.

"I know it's hard, baby, but try not to let it get to you. Trust me, I feel your pain. The threats alone have my mind whirling twenty-four seven."

"Wait... you didn't tell me you received threats."

He nodded. "I've had a few men in my inbox, threatening me. Some saying if that was their sister, they would've done this or that. It's a mess.

I just turned my settings to send anyone I don't follow to the message request box."

I grabbed his face gently. "God will fix this. He will."

He shrugged. "Okay. But back to you. What did you mean by your father saying something you've been thinking about?"

I crossed my legs under me. "He said, 'I had a life planned out for you and you threw it away, for what? An unstable career in one of the darkest industries known to man.' While I don't agree with him trying to plan my life, I've been thinking about how unstable this industry is."

I thought through what I was about to say next. "Did I ever tell you I had a dream of launching a loungewear brand? I also wanted to have my own shoe line."

He smiled. "Really?"

"Really. So, I was praying after my father left, asking God if I was doing the music thing out of rebellion or because I really wanted to."

"And?"

I looked down at my hands, then allowed my eyes to meet his again. "I think it's both. A part of me wanted to show my father he couldn't run me, but I also never expected to fall in love with the music industry the way I did. The internship continued to open doors for me, and I realized I had a gift."

His phone went off this time. He answered, then stood up.

"It's our food. I'll go down and grab it real quick."

My stomach growled. I was glad he had ordered on his way to my place, because I had no desire to cook or any desire to eat what I had in the fridge. While I waited for him to come back up, I thought about what I'd shared with him. This wasn't the first time I'd been thinking about changing careers, or at least, adding to my portfolio. My father's words just made me think about it harder.

The truth was, this industry was unstable. Look how quickly we'd lost two artists and how easily people could blackball you. While I was definitely doing good financially and would continue to reap the benefits of my time in the industry due to royalties, I wondered if God was pushing me into something else.

My door chime went off as Shane re-entered my condo.

"Oh my gosh, it smells so good," I said, standing up.

"No. Relax. I'll make you a plate and bring it to you."

Sitting back down, I couldn't believe my excitement at the sight of some of my favorite comfort foods. Pizza, wings and fries. Shane handed me a tray, then set my food down. He poured me a glass of ginger ale, then went and fixed his plate. Once he was settled next to me, I blessed the food, then continued.

"I don't think I'm ready to quit, but I'm definitely ready to put some other things in place."

"I get that," he said, biting into his pizza. "It's kind of like me and the coffee shop. We know that time in the entertainment world may not last forever."

"Exactly. So, once we can breathe again and all this is over, I'll see what God says."

He kissed my greasy lips. "Whatever you need, I'm here. As long as you know I got you."

"Based on all this good food, I would say you have me for sure."

Twenty-Three

SHANE

2 weeks later

I RUSHED THROUGH THE TURNSTILE, nearly knocking down a woman as I headed for the elevator.

"I'm so sorry, ma'am," I said before the doors shut.

I hit floor number nine. I tried catching my breath and composing myself before I reached my attorney's office. He'd gotten a break in the case and really believed it would make Remi drop the charges and it would clear my name. Finally, the elevator chimed, and I stepped off. I hurried into his office, waiting until the receptionist told me he was ready for me.

"Mr. Bishop," he said, greeting me with a bro hug. "Today just might be your lucky day."

"I hope so," I said. "Sean, what happened?"

He shut his door, then we both sat down. My leg shook as I waited for him to speak. He pulled out a recorder instead.

"When you were in the bathroom, did you guys hear anything outside the door? Anything at all? Footsteps?"

I shook my head. "No. I mean, the upstairs of Kevell's home is fully carpeted. You couldn't hear anyone walking unless they were stomping like crazy."

He pressed play on the recorder.

"I know I should've said something sooner, but I was scared. I didn't want to get involved and I don't want to testify," I heard a female voice say.

"Just tell us what you saw and what you heard." That was my attorney's voice.

I heard a deep breath, then the female voice again.

"I was upstairs, making out with one of the players from the team. We used one of the bedrooms right next to the bathroom. When we were leaving, I heard some voices in the bathroom. The player I was with was afraid someone would see us, so he covered my mouth."

"Is there a reason he didn't want anyone to see you guys?"

Silence. "He's married."

My mouth fell open.

"Okay. Continue."

"I heard a female voice say, 'Oh, what's wrong? You can't have a little fun while Wifey

is out of town'. Then I heard her say, nobody has to know."

I almost fell out of my chair. All this time, somebody had heard what happened in the bathroom. I couldn't believe one of my teammates would leave me out to dry just because he didn't want his wife to know he was a dog.

"What happened next? Did you hear anything else?"

"The last thing I heard was him say he wouldn't touch her, but that was it. I swear, that's all I heard."

"Can you please confirm the date and time you heard this and tell us who you believe the voices belonged to?"

"Yes. It was August twentieth around 11:30 p.m. I know it was Shane's voice and I'm guessing the girl was Remi."

Sean stopped the recorder. "That was our witness, Shannon Carpenter. She was making out with your buddy, Hakim Richards."

"Hakim?"

I couldn't believe it. Hakim and I weren't that close, but he was always a pretty decent guy. He was also more religious than me.

"Yep. We verified the story with him and while he's asking us not to include him, sadly, we'll have to," Sean said, folding his hands on his desk. "We need all the witnesses we can get to corroborate your side of the story. Him backing up Shannon is perfect."

I stared at Sean, trying to wrap my mind around what I'd just heard. For the last six weeks, I'd been asking God to make a way out of no way. I begged Him to clear my name. All this time, there were two people who could've helped clear my name, but they didn't.

"Why now? Clearly, his wife will find out once this goes public?" I asked.

"Let's just say, she's not the only one he's cheating on his wife with. A woman scorned is the greatest asset to us lawyers in cases like this."

"A woman scorned is what got me into this mess."

I was still processing this whole thing. I was grateful and couldn't wait to tell Essence.

"So, what's next?"

"Well, we have her statement on record. If we can't get Hakim's right now, we have enough to take to Remi and her attorney. I'm sure this alone will make her drop it. But, if we can get Hakim, it'll be better. Either way, you're about to get your life back."

I finally relaxed my shoulders and sat back against the chair. "Man, this wasn't luck. This was nothing but God."

* * *

"MR. BISHOP, how do you feel now that the charges have been dropped and you've been reinstated to play with your team?"

Camera lights flashed around me and the sound of reporters clicking their pens surrounded me. I looked to my right, where my family and Essence stood, before I responded.

"I feel like God heard my cries. I've never painted myself as perfect, but I've always been an honest and upstanding man. I'm excited to get back into the groove of life."

"Are you upset your coach didn't take your side?"

I looked into the audience at my coach and my teammates, who had come to support me.

"I understand he had to do what he needed to protect the team and hold me accountable. I'm upset that we have a system in place where a man loses everything before he's even tried in a court of law, but it is what it is."

I looked over as a female reporter raised her hand.

"Yes. Kim. I can't see your nametag, sorry if I messed that up," I said.

"It's Kia. No worries. I don't think that's how you should look at it. 'It is what it is' is the exact thinking that has some of our promising young athletes get accused and end up losing scholarships or getting expelled from a great college because of an accusation. What's your take on that?"

I looked over at Essence again. She winked.

"You're right, but I wanted to be careful how I address this. Women should always be protected, and if they have been sexually assaulted, then the person responsible should be held accountable to the fullest letter of the law." I caught my breath. "But to Kia's point, there are so many young athletes that don't have a witness who heard or saw anything. It's unfortunate that we don't have better laws in place for this, but maybe one day we will."

A white male raised his hand. "What would you say to those young athletes?"

I stared at the big light that was set up in the back. After a few seconds, I cleared my throat.

"If you know you're innocent, trust God to send the ram in the bush when you need it most."

My publicist stepped forward. "Okay, okay. One last question, then we'll have to go. Thank you."

A white woman in the back raised her hand.

"Yes."

"With all that's going on, how does it feel to have your family standing by your side today? I know things were probably strained with the truth about your father not being your biological father."

I gripped the edges of the podium. We were honestly still working through that, but I had to say something.

"To be honest, we're still working through everything, but what I can say is that it takes a lot for a man to stand up and raise another man's child." I looked over at my dad. "I guess you can say, there were two innocent people in this situation. Him and I."

More reporters raised their hands, but my publicist pushed me away from the podium. "That's enough. Thank you again."

She rushed me off stage with my family. I hated press conferences, but it felt good to clear my name. This was a huge win in my book.

My father walked over to me once we were backstage. "Thanks, Son. That meant a lot."

I grabbed his shoulders. "Well, it's true. I'm still hurt, and I'm not saying I understand why you guys lied, but I can appreciate that you were wounded in all of this as well, and you just wanted to protect me."

He nodded. "I love you."

At the sound of his voice cracking, I almost lost it. I grabbed him in a bear hug. My mother stood behind him, dabbing the corner of her eyes. Once we parted ways, I hugged my mother and sister. Essence waited patiently.

"Come here, you," I said.

"I'm proud of you, babe," she responded, throwing her arms around my neck. "That line about God was so good."

My dad nodded. "I agree."

"I'm just glad this is all over," Sahana said. "Your lawyer earned a bonus."

We all laughed. This was the first time in months I didn't have to force myself to laugh or find joy. I was genuinely happy. We walked toward the SUV that was waiting for us. I hired a chef to make a big celebratory dinner for us back at my place. I didn't want to go out, and while I appreciated all the love on social media over the last few days, since the truth had come out, I just wanted to be with my family. We piled into the truck, then waited as my publicist and a few officers cleared away the press that surrounded the truck.

"I'll call you tomorrow," she said. "Go."

The driver pulled off just as a female reporter and her cameraman stepped out of the way. Once we made it a few blocks away from where the press conference was held, Sahana spoke.

"While I'm glad she did, I can't believe Remi dropped the charges just like that."

I loosened my tie. "It wasn't much she could do or say. None of us expected for somebody to be passing the bathroom, let alone, because they weren't supposed to be up there, that they would hear most of our conversation."

"Talk about a ram in the bush," my mother joked.

"Listen, I hate Hakim cheated on his wife, but I'm grateful Shannon decided to help. I don't care that she waited; I get her not wanting a target on her back."

Sahana scrolled through her phone. "Target is right. Even with how she helped you, everyone is coming at her on social for being a home wrecker and for waiting so long. Social media is brutal."

I shook my head. I hated it for that very reason, but in today's world, this was how everybody got their news and kept up on the latest trends. I wanted to reach out to Shannon and let her know, if she needed anything, I would try to help, but my attorney told me it was best to let everything blow over first.

"When did Coach say you could play your first game?"

I looked at Essence. "I told him I wanted to play in the season opener."

My mother turned around in her seat. "But you missed training camp."

"But I never stopped training."

My father, who was in the front seat, looked at me through the rearview mirror. "That's my boy."

I winked.

"Whenever we were at his place, he was out there, everyday training like he knew he was going to play," Essence said. "Commitment looks good on you, boo."

"That's funny, but it does. In every way."

I grabbed her and kissed her.

"Well, let's get to this seafood dinner you've been bragging about," Sahana said. "I'm starving."

I rested my head against the headrest. Closing my eyes, I absorbed the silence. I'd gotten a lot of rest in the last two weeks. Training had me tired, which worked in my favor since I hadn't slept the first month when all of this went down. All I could do was relish in this moment. I knew God would provide, I just didn't know how. Now, I was grateful I hadn't ignored Him when He told me to practice and to keep believing. I had passed the test.

ESSENCE

FINALLY, Trish and I were sitting down to discuss our new vision for the label and management company. Now that things were slowly getting back to normal, and all the commotion had died down, we could focus on where we were headed. We had Winter Daze, May Reed and Majestic Hits remaining, but this was actually a good thing. Winter working with Dev Hits caused her album to be the most requested R&B Soul album this quarter and it was being released in November, just in time for the holiday push.

Majestic had also been teaming up with Dev Hits, not only to work on Winter's album, but also helping him with some of his other artists. Since he was signed to us, we got a percentage of the profits and May Reed had just written a few songs for some heavy hitters and was seeing money before her album was even done. Trish and I feared things would crash and burn once Remi accused Shane and left our label, but it seemed that because this was such a constant in the industry, some people knew to wait it out.

I hated that throughout the last six weeks, people accused me of not caring about women, being a rapist lover, and being more concerned about money than people. I'd lost much sleep behind this. While I knew it came with the territory, I was burned out physically and mentally. Shane and I wanted to take a vacation, but since the season was in full swing, we had to find the time in our busy schedules.

"I can't believe how God turned this situation around," Trish said, disrupting my deep thinking. "Even after losing two people, we're still on track to end this quarter and this year very well. The songwriting has definitely been our bread and butter."

"Yeah, I saw that. I feel like that's our sweet spot," I said, typing away on my laptop. "So, what do you say? I think we can chill on signing new people for a while. Let's make stars out of the ones we have and continue to strengthen their songwriting skills."

Trish nodded. "You know what's crazy? I was thinking that after we brought Remi on. Even before she started showing her diva ways, I felt like we were good."

I loved when Trish and I agreed. It was hard having a business partner at times, but 80 percent of the time, we literally thought the same thing.

"Great. So, I'll have to let this new artist that sent me over their profile and information know we're putting things on hold for a while."

Trish nodded. "Besides, I really hope we both pursue the other things God placed in our hearts. It's time we did some things for us."

Trish had always known about my dreams of owning a loungewear apparel line. She'd also shared with me her desire to launch her own magazine. We were definitely women who had a heart to help others, but it was time for us to start pursuing our own dreams.

"So, what's our timeframe, sis? Two years?"

I leaned back in my chair and thought for a second. "I would say, let's pray and fast about it. Let God give us a time. However, we can start preparing now. I'm sure there's a whole process I need to learn about before I hire a designer, and you certainly need to write the business plan for your magazine."

"The excitement got to me," she said, laughing. "Let's do it. Fast and pray, then let God lead us."

I grabbed her hand and gave it a gentle squeeze. "Isn't that how we built this business?"

Nodding, she smiled at me with tears in her eyes. "This journey has been tiring and overwhelming, but fun and fulfilling at the same time. I went from being an artist, to a full-time manager and songwriter. I couldn't have done it without you."

All I could do was smile to keep from crying. Trish was right. As two black women in the music industry, we'd had our shares of ups and downs, often experiencing more downs than anything. We wanted to give up so many times over the last five years, but God wouldn't let us. I knew He would guide us to our end date for Taylor Made Music Group. For now, we would continue to sow and reap the reward for our hard work.

* * *

"MOM, WHERE ARE YOU?" I yelled, entering my parents' home for the first time in what felt like months.

My mom and I had been meeting up once a week, either for brunch or dinner, but we spent most of our time out of the house, mostly when my father was out of town for a preaching gig or when he was too busy to spend time with her. Today, we were having brunch here at the house since he would be away for most of the day.

"Hey, dear. I was just finishing my makeup," she said, coming down the steps. "You look gorgeous."

Smiling, I met her at the bottom of the stairs, and we embraced. These hugs had been monumental in me getting through the last six weeks of drama. I held on for a bit longer, then stepped back.

"So, do you."

"Your father left out about an hour ago," she continued. "I hate this tension between you two, but I told him he needed to listen to you and stop wanting to hear himself talk so much."

I forced a smile. I appreciated that she had my back, but I had too many positive things going on for me now and I didn't need the negative energy.

"Dad will always be dad. How's your back?"

"It's better. Much better."

I eyed her carefully. I thought about how Shane told me he had to always ask his dad about his health, but the automatic response was always, 'I'm fine'. I had to trust what she said, since there was no way of knowing, but I promised myself I was going to her next appointment. One thing about my father, he stayed on top of her about her health. I just hoped her 'I'm fine' was the truth.

"You have no idea how relieved I am that all of this stuff got worked out. I was praying hard," she said as we headed into the kitchen. "I made all your favorites."

I walked over to the stove and took the lid off one of the pots. "Hmmm, you know how much I love seafood okra."

She pushed me to the side to take the biscuits out of the oven. "These were all set, just warming a little."

I helped her set the food on the table, which included cheese grits, turkey bacon and a fruit salad. I knew she should probably eat a healthier meal, but I had to admit, when we went out to eat, she stuck to chicken or fish and vegetables for her sides. A soul food brunch here and there couldn't hurt. After she blessed the food, we dug in.

"So, I wanted to share something with you," she started, pouring herself some water. "I reached out to First Lady Bishop and we'll be having lunch next week."

I dropped my fork. "Really? Were you nice?"

She flagged me off playfully. "Stop. I'm a sweetheart."

I raised my eyebrow. "Mom, the way you treated that woman years back at that conference in Miami was horrible. You basically made her feel like she was beneath you."

She stuffed bacon into her mouth. After chewing for a few seconds, she responded. "I know, I know. I felt horrible. Trust me when I tell you God has been dealing with me heavily. I wanted to reach out to her once you and I had a groove and I knew you had found a groove with Shane, but then, all this drama happened. I didn't want her to think I was trying to be nosy."

I picked my fork back up and continued to eat. "Yeah, that was wise. I'm sure she was shocked to hear your voice."

"Actually, she was happy to hear it. I guess with our children dating, she figured it was time we really got to know one another. I apologized for my behavior at the conference and offered to treat her to lunch."

It was crazy that things were working themselves out. Shane had taken my mother out a few times and they had a blast getting to know one another, but he admitted it was awkward that our mothers weren't building a bond. He knew my mother had an air about her, but he also knew she was easier to deal with than my father. I was grateful the ladies would set the family affair off. The fellas could catch up whenever my father came to his senses.

"So, Baby Girl, how's your heart? I know you said you're glad everything is over, but you and I both know over doesn't mean there won't be some residue left behind."

"You're speaking truth, Mama. I still get comments on my social. Even with proof, people feel like they have to stick to their original opinion because humility is so hard these days." I took a few sips of my water. "But, since I started going to therapy again when all this jumped off, it's really helped me put a strategy in place to handle those things."

"That's good. I'm still praying about therapy. I know it'll be good for me on a personal level, but I really don't want to go without your father."

I nodded. I could understand that. Even Shane and I had done a few sessions with his therapist together, just to work through the drama and even some relationship stuff. It had been good for us.

"Well, with the way God is working on your heart, I'm sure as you continue to pray, He'll turn Daddy's heart. If anyone can do it, He can."

My mother grabbed my hand. "Oh, baby, I hope so. I'm trying not to lose faith, but that father of yours is so stubborn."

I continued eating in silence. She didn't have to convince me who my father was. I knew firsthand. I was wondering if she was reaping the harvest of letting him control so much of our lives. Being a man in his late fifties, he probably didn't think he needed to change. She should've nipped it in a bud, especially when I was younger. Either way, I had her back. I'd been fasting and praying like crazy in this season. The chains would break soon enough. They had to.

Twenty-Four

SHANE

I WATCHED as Casey walked closer to the picnic table I was sitting on. I wasn't sure whether to stand up and hug her, or just let this play out as normal as possible. I was sure she felt just as awkward as I did. Here it was, just a few weeks after we'd found out the truth of who leaked the news, and we were about to have another discussion that could change everything for us. I was still wrestling with whether I needed to, or even wanted to, have a relationship with her, but today would be a start.

"Hey," she said, sitting next to me. "Fall is slowly coming in."

"Sorry about that," I said. "I realized meeting in a park in October may not have been the greatest idea."

She shrugged. "No worries. This is my favorite season."

We both stared straight ahead, with minutes passing before either of us spoke again.

"Listen, I'm sorry for accusing you of leaking the story. I didn't know who to believe or who I could trust."

She finally looked at me. "Shane, none of this has been easy. I even thought it could be my mother."

I smirked, thinking about how Sahana had said the same thing.

"Well, it felt good to know it wasn't family," I said. "It just sucks to know that somebody I did trust could do me dirty."

After doing some research and tracking down a few leads, Sean was able to find out that it was Nick who had leaked the story to the press. He thought using a burner phone would cover his tracks, but sadly, the convenience store had his face on camera, buying the burner phone and the place where he met the reporter also had his face on camera. As discrete as he thought he had been, he wasn't.

"I can't believe people think NDAs are just something celebrities use to trick them into being quiet," I continued. "They're legal documents that can get you sued if you break them."

"So, is that what you're going to do? Sue Nick?"

I let out a deep breath. "I kind of want to put this behind me and move on, but a part of me wants him to pay. Do you know he only got $10,000 for the story? Like, was it even worth it?"

She chuckled. "That's sad. Just goes to show that people will do anything for money."

I looked at her.

"I'm just glad you realize that that's not me," she continued. "I genuinely want to build a relationship with you, but I've come to the conclusion that I'll have closure either way. I've done my part."

The tears in her eyes melted my heart. I felt crazy because I wanted a relationship with her, too, but a part of me felt like I would be betraying Sahana. It was weird how many emotions came over me whenever I thought about this situation. Sahana was actually encouraging me to get to know Casey and build with her.

"I think I'm scared," I said. "Scared that building with you will be betraying them. I know that's not true, but it's what I think about."

She relaxed her arms, holding onto the table's edge with her hands. "You know, I know how that feels. My mother feels betrayed every time I mention you. She feels like our father betrayed her, and seeing us together would keep reminding her of that."

I thought about how Casey was risking a lot to build a relationship with me.

"Then why do it?"

She wiped a tear from her eye. "I told you. All I have is my mom.

THE ESSENCE OF HIS SOUL

She's not that close to her family and I need more than just her. You ever feel like there's a piece of you missing, but you can't quite put your finger on it?"

I nodded. I'd been feeling that way since Samuel died. I missed my brother every day.

"I do. My situation is a little different, but I understand where you're coming from."

I held my hand out. She looked down, then looked back at me. I nodded. She grabbed my hand.

"I would love to build a relationship with you," I said. "I just ask that you be patient with me. I'm still processing it all and working through things with my parents."

She broke down crying and I wrapped her in a hug. She didn't want my money or clout. She honestly just wanted to build a bond with me. I felt it when she spoke and even now, as I held her hand, I knew she was being genuine. One of the traumas of being a celebrity was that you had to drill everyone who came into your life to make sure they were on the up and up.

"Thanks, Shane. That means a lot," she whispered as I continued to hold her hand.

I thought about my birth father and what this moment would've meant for him. I also wondered if he were still alive, would we be having this moment? It was because of him not being here that Casey felt led to do some digging, and here we were. Maybe it wasn't meant for me to figure out all the 'what ifs', but I was certainly going to lean into what was.

* * *

I GRABBED her hand and helped her step down from the carriage. We'd only been able to do a few horse and carriage rides throughout the city over the summer, but I wanted to sneak one more in before the fall really hit. We were still getting seventy and eighty-degree days, so today was perfect. I had one more surprise I had to pull off before it got cold, but I had been planning that for weeks, and had no worries at all.

"Thanks, babe."

I grabbed her around the waist and led her down Chestnut Street. Old City was one of my favorite neighborhoods, which was why I chose it as a location for Mocha Tea & Trends.

"This is a beautiful day to stroll through the city."

"It is. It's nice to see people smiling at me instead of scowling at me."

"I would laugh, but I think it's too soon for us to laugh about it."

I moved over for a lady and her dog. "I've been laughing. Sometimes, you gotta laugh to keep from crying."

"What makes you want to cry?"

"The fact that it's always going to be there, even though I'm innocent. When you Google my name, this will come up."

On her silence, I decided to cross the street. My favorite ice cream shop was on that side.

"That's the frustrating part," she finally responded. "But we made it through."

I opened the door and she stepped inside. We made our way into the ice cream shop, placing our orders at the counter. As we waited, she played with my goatee, making me laugh. I looked into her eyes, finding the serenity I always found when I looked at her. This was why I knew marrying her was the right decision. She was my safe space and my muse all at the same time.

"Don't think I wasn't paying attention. The way you handled all of this with grace leaves me speechless."

She sighed. "I mean, it was definitely a test of my faith, but it taught me not to run for cover."

"Here you both go," the cashier said, handing us our cones.

We found a table and sat down.

"So, how do you feel now that you've decided to build a relationship with Casey?"

I licked my ice cream, letting the sweet taste of butter almond melt in my mouth. "After actually saying it out loud and hanging with her yesterday, I feel really good about it. One day at a time, ya know?"

She nodded. "That's all any of us can do. One day at a time with everything."

"If there was one thing you would want to happen for you before this year is out, what would it be?"

"That's pretty deep," she said. "I guess that everyone around me would heal so our relationships would be better."

I thought about what she said. I knew she was referring to her father, but I also knew that she and her mother were still working through some things.

"I would want to spend the rest of my life with you," I said without hesitation. "That's the way I would love to end my year."

As much as she tried, she couldn't hold back her smile. Blushing, she licked the ice cream from around her lips. "Are you serious?"

"Yes. Very."

"Well, make it happen."

I laughed as we continued eating our ice cream. She had no idea I was about to do just that.

* * *

I WALKED as close as I could to the water without freaking out. My therapist and I had worked through some exercises to help me overcome my fears, but I wasn't ready to go buy a yacht just yet. I turned back, taking in the setup. The lights that streamed across the top created a beautiful ambiance. The band was set up nicely, with the pianist lightly playing the keys as I waited for her family to arrive. She was scheduled to arrive in an hour, and I wanted everything to go perfectly.

"Mr. Bishop, I believe her father is here," one of the waitresses said, stopping in front of me with a tray of wings. "I know you didn't want anyone to disturb you prior to the proposal, but he wants to talk to you."

I looked at her face. I could tell by how fast she spoke that he had rattled her. I'd learned enough from Essence to know that he probably made most people shake under his presence. I couldn't believe this would be the first time we were actually meeting.

"I'll talk to him," I said. "Thanks."

Before heading toward the area where our families would be seated, I whispered a quick prayer. I touched my pants pocket, feeling for the ring box. I tried asking for her hand in marriage, but he refused to meet with me. I asked her mother and figured she would deal with her father. Making my way toward the front of the pier, I took long strides and kept my head held high.

"Shane," he said, as soon as we were face to face."

"Bishop Taylor," I said, holding my hand out.

He grabbed it and shook it. Firmly. There was silence between us, then we both went to speak at the same time.

"You first, sir," I said.

He looked down at the water, then back at me. "You know, Essence was supposed to be a boy. That's what the doctors told us, but they were wrong."

I tried not to respond. She told me how she knew that was one of his issues. It saddened me to think a man could be so cold toward his daughter because she wasn't the son he longed for.

He cleared his throat. "She was always a leader, knew what she wanted from a young age. I saw the defiance and stubbornness the minute she came out of the womb."

"Like father, like daughter."

He chuckled. "I guess I deserve that. Listen, I don't hate you, I just don't understand my daughter's choices. But I realize I have to respect them if I want to be a part of her life. It frightens me to think I could miss out on the rest of her life or even my future grandchildren's life because I haven't been able to honor my daughter properly."

I listened intently. Maybe that was why he'd been calling. For the last several weeks, Essence and I had been spending as much time together as possible, especially with me being smack dab in the height of the season. She declined many of his calls, not willing to talk to him after their last argument. Now, I wondered if he had been trying to make amends.

"My father was hard," he continued. "Very. I had no choice but to go into ministry. At least not if I wanted to stay in his will. It's crazy how much I preach on breaking generational curses, only to be repeating them."

He wiped at his eye. I had never seen Bishop Taylor this vulnerable. Whenever I saw him preaching on television or whenever our family's ministries crossed paths, he was always sturdy and strong.

"Bishop, I appreciate you sharing your heart with me but I think Essence should hear this. I'm not the one you should apologize to."

"Well, I've been trying, but I understand why she's ignoring my calls. I'm hoping today, I can make amends. If that's okay with you. I don't want to disrupt this moment."

I eyed him carefully. I heard the sincerity in his voice.

"Only on one condition."

He squared his shoulders. "What's that?"

I reached into my pocket and pulled out the ring. "May I please have your daughter's hand in marriage?"

He choked up but caught himself. "Yes. Of course. Wow. I can't believe this day is here."

He wiped at his eye again, and I patted him on the back. I wanted to hug him, but I figured he didn't even want me to sense he was having a moment. Just when I was about to speak again, Winter walked over.

"Hey, sorry to interrupt, but Trish just called and said they will be here in thirty minutes," she said. "Bishop Taylor, it's a pleasure to meet you."

She shook his hand.

"My pleasure," he said.

I turned to look over everything one last time. "She's a little early. Why is Trish bringing her so soon?"

"Something about Essence catching onto something she said, and she thinks she'll figure it out. The longer you wait, the more questions she'll ask."

"Got it. Well, who's here?"

"Everyone's back in the family area you set up. I think we're just waiting for a few of her industry friends you invited. That's it."

I smiled. "You ready to blow?"

"I'm ready. I got you, bro. I promise."

I nodded as she headed toward the family area.

"Bishop Taylor," I said, turning back to my future father-in-law. "Shall we?"

He smiled. "We shall."

As we walked back inside, I couldn't help but think about how I'd been able to make amends with two men who would be in my life forever. While I had never met my biological father, I could appreciate that I now had double for my trouble. I wasn't thinking Bishop Taylor and I would be best friends, but having two Godly men to help me navigate this crazy world was a blessing for sure.

* * *

"HOW DID you pull this off without me knowing a thing?" she asked, eyeing her ring for the hundredth time. "And this ring... Babe, it's gorgeous."

I kissed her. "I have my ways. I can't believe you almost figured it out."

I twirled her around again as everyone looked on. The proposal had gone off without a hitch. I realized this was only the third time I'd seen my woman cry since we'd been together. I clearly had her beat in that department, and while I didn't want to ever see her crying unless they were tears of joy, the vulnerability she showed tonight made me realize that the right person could help you step into your true self.

"Well, Trish was very careful, so don't be mad at her, but I'm very smart. I just thought you were throwing me a surprise party for being nominated for the ASCAP Songwriter of the Year Award. I never would've guessed engagement."

"I wanted you to think that," I teased. "It was perfect timing, and by the way... we're celebrating that, too."

I turned her around and pointed toward the ice sculpture the waiters were bringing out. It was a sculpture of the award with her name at the bottom.

"I know you'll win, but if they decide to let politics get in the way, you'll always be a winner in my eyes."

She covered her face with her hands, then slowly walked over.

"This is too much," she said. "If I don't win, this is enough for me."

We embraced, with me snuggling my face in her neck. At the sound of her giggling, I pulled her back to the dance floor. She looked around.

"You didn't invite Casey?"

"Actually, I did. She's a pretty decent person. She didn't want me to feel uncomfortable with everyone staring at her or wondering about our relationship. She wanted me to enjoy the evening with you. We'll link up soon."

She nodded. "She definitely has your heart."

I dipped her back, then pulled her back up. When I did, I noticed her smile fading away.

"Uh, can I butt in, please?"

When I heard her father's voice, I pulled away from her. "Sure."

She grabbed my hand, pulling me back. "Can this wait?"

I hadn't told her about our conversation. One, I had no time, but more importantly, he wasn't going to get me to do his dirty work. He needed to let her hear those words from him.

"Please. I come in peace."

She looked at me. I winked, then kissed her cheek. "Talk to your father."

Letting out a deep sigh, she took his hand and started dancing with him. I looked at the DJ and gave a nod. He switched the song to something more befitting. I walked away to give them some privacy. I wanted to hear what was going on, but I knew she would fill me in. I only had two days before I was back on the road, so I had every plan to spend all tomorrow with her.

I walked around the pier, greeting everyone else. Once I saw them hugging, I turned to our families.

"Everybody on the dance floor," I said, waving my hands. "Let's go. No wallflowers around here."

My teammates who were able to make it grabbed some ladies in the room and started dancing as the DJ played "Let Me Clear My Throat". As Maurice and Trish got on the dance floor, I walked over to them.

"Sis, thank you for everything. This was everything I envisioned."

"Anything for my sister. Thank you for loving her right and," she said, looking over, "for showing her it's okay to open her heart up."

We both looked up as her father wiped the tears that flowed down her face.

"Hey, that's my job," I teased.

Trish popped my arm. "Really? Let them have their moment."

Laughing, I slowly walked over, trying to gauge if it was time to step back in. Just then, Sahana grabbed my hands and whirled me around.

"Dance with me," she said, getting into the groove of the music.

We danced for a few minutes, then I danced with my mother, Essence's mother, and Trish. I was ready to dance with my baby again. Finally, we were standing in front of each other.

"You know what I realized?" she said, as I took her in my arms again.

I kissed her shoulder gently. "What?"

"We're at a pier."

I looked into her eyes. "And?"

"The water," she said softly.

"Well, therapy will cause you to take baby steps to get over your fears."

We stared at each other. "Did you do this for me? I would've gladly taken a sidewalk proposal."

We shared a laugh. "I did it for me. At some point, we'll take a cruise. Probably in about five years, but the pier was the right setting. Water speaks to life and new beginnings."

She nodded. "It does. It seems like new beginnings are happening all around us."

I paused. "Wait. I'm slowly getting over my fears, but what about yours? How do we work on that?"

She sighed. "I think we already have. Remember when I told you that my safety had been compromised because of that moment?"

"Of course, I remember."

"Well, for the last seven months, you've created a safe place for me emotionally, mentally, physically, and spiritually. Getting over my fears doesn't mean I have to stand under fireworks."

I stared into her eyes. "I got the beauty and the brains. Love it. So, what about your father?"

"Babe, I've never seen him so vulnerable and open. He shared things from his childhood that I never knew about. So much pain."

I took in what she said. "Isn't it funny how in seven months, we both had some kind of falling out with our families, then realized that God was using it for our good? If you hadn't entered my life, I'm not sure I would've been able to get through this."

"We definitely drew closer to one another, even when we thought we were losing our families."

"Tell me one lesson you learned from all of this," I said. "I have mine, but you go first."

She looked up at the sky, then back at me. "Love is worth fighting for."

I nodded. "Good one. I would say, God will always fight for you, you need only to be still."

"Hmmmm, that's a great one."

Kissing her again, this time with a little tongue, I pulled her into me. "I would go through all of this again just to get to this point with you."

"Now, that's love," she teased.

We continued dancing, allowing the music and the night's energy to take over our bodies. I closed my eyes as we slowed it down and she laid her head on my shoulder. I meant what I said. The last seven months had been hell, but it led me to this moment with her and I had no regrets. As I opened my eyes again, taking in the room, I smiled. No regrets at all.

About the Author

Born and raised in North Philadelphia, Mya K. Douglas, professionally known as Mya Kay, is an Amazon best-selling author, speaker and literary consultant. She was a semi-finalist for America's Next Great Author, a reality show dedicated to giving writers a seat at the table. She has written and co-written several Christian/contemporary romance novels, including, *The Storms of Love* series, *Love to the B Power, Love to the Baby Power, Fumbled Your Heart* and *A Star-Studded Love*. Her devotional, *The God Girl's Guide to College Life*, was #1 in new releases on Amazon during the week of its release. Mya is also the creator and co-host of "The Writing Bar Podcast", with Nailah Harvey, a new writing podcast that features tips and tools for writers who are looking for ways to monetize their writing and build a following without compromising their faith. You can learn more about her work at http://www.writermya.com and be sure to follow her on social @writermya on all platforms.

Other Books by Mya Kay

<u>Storms of Love</u>

Battles of Love

In Loving Bliss

Fumbled Your Heart

Love to the B Power

Love to the Baby Power

<u>A Star-Studded Love</u>

Thank You

Thanks for reading! If you enjoyed this book, please leave a review on Amazon and mark it as read on Goodreads. We hate errors but they do happen. If you catch any, please send them to us directly at <u>blovepublications@gmail.com</u> with ERRORS as the subject.

Love publications
Heart Piercing Swoon Worthy Black Love Stories

Made in the USA
Las Vegas, NV
29 January 2025